Viking Kids Don't Cry

Ieda Jónasdóttir Herman

Paperback ISBN: 978-0-9982816-8-1

Ísafjörður
Eyjafjörður
Dalvik
Vopnafjörður
Akureyri
Lake
Lagarfljót
Stykkishólmur
Iceland
Reyðarfjörður
Djúpivogur
Reykjavík
Höfn
Westman
Islands
Vik

TABLE OF CONTENTS

CHAPTER 1

The Trölls are Coming! The Trölls are Coming!

Ten-year-old Didda and her nine-year old sister, Lilla, sat outside the infirmary that Aunt Thora and Uncle Olaf ran. The adults were inside now busy taking care of fishermen who had nearly drowned in the bay earlier in the week.

"I don't think I want to go to Grandpa's farm this year." Lilla said, shaking her curly head. She chewed on a blade of grass and rubbed her left toe in the black lava sand.

"What?" Didda's head jerked up. "Why not?" she demanded as she impatiently brushed a dark-brown strand of hair from her freckled nose.

"I just don't like the chickens, or that wicked rooster, or any of those mean cows with their stupid sharp horns," Lilla frowned. "I'll just stay here. You go and help Sissi with the work."

Didda was silent as she looked around. The large house had an infirmary annex where staff tended the less-critical patients. The medical staff airlifted any patients with major injuries to a larger hospital.

Several white flour-sacks hung on a clothesline had moved slightly in the soft breeze. Over by the tall cliffs were two rusty corrugated sheds, the once-white paint faded to a non-descript gray. Uncle Olaf used one shed to store rakes, scythes and other tools needed to keep what little grass was able to grow. The other held seldom-used bridles and saddles. Their uncle and aunt stayed busy with sick or injured folks at the infirmary and did not ride very often.

It was nice there, but Didda thought there was so much more to do and explore at Grandpa's. She reached down and selected a broad leaf of grass. Putting it between her left and right thumb she gave a hearty blow, the piercing squeal gave most satisfactory noise that scared up a flock of seagulls. The scowl left Lilla's face as the two sisters grinned at each other.

Didda squinted as she watched one bird standing on a large lava rock. She stood and stomped her foot to see how it would take off. The bird glided up into the air, its wings spread wide and its feet tucked tight under its body.

"Hey Lilla, I have an idea. If we put those flour-sacks on our arms like wings, I bet we could fly, just like those sea gulls up there."

Didda watched as it gracefully swept in a curve, and came in for a landing on another rock a short distance away. Didda could see its webbed yellow feet come down straight and watched as the bird hopped a bit before settling down.

"Did you see that? We can do that," Didda hollered. "See? We can climb to the top of the shed, tie the sacks onto our neck, and then just spread our arms out like wings. When we jump, we pull up our knees, just like the birds do their legs. We just jump from the top of one shed to the other and we'll be flying."

Didda clambered down, excited. She stopped when she realized her sister was not following. "Come on Lilla, this will be fun. Grandpa and Sissi will be here later and we can show them how we can fly."

Didda was already climbing. Without warning, small rocks began to rain down from the cliff behind the sheds.

"No, no, come down! The roof is shaking!" Lilla shrieked.

Didda felt the shed sway. She heard clattering, as rocks pelted the corrugated roof and sides of the structure. Frantically, Didda scrambled back down yelling to her sister.

"Run Lilla, run, it's an earthquake, the trölls are coming!" Then both ran awkwardly, the ground moving under their feet. It was as if they were on the deck of a ship in a stormy gale. They ran weaving and screaming hysterically. "The trölls are coming, the trölls are coming."

As they neared the house, Aunt Thora and Uncle Olaf came running. Aunt Thora reach to hug Lilla, trying to calm her down. The ground continued to roll as if a giant monster-worm was crawling under their feet.

"This is just a little tremor, an earthquake. The center of the quake is miles away." Uncle Olaf said soothingly.

"What on earth do you mean 'the trölls are coming'?" Aunt Thora asked as they hurried into the house.

Didda looked around cautiously. A few pictures were hanging crookedly on the walls. A spoon, two forks and a cup had bounced off the table. The cup was rocking gently on the floor. A small rivulet of coffee ran across the wood floor from the upside down black enameled coffeepot.

"What was that? What's happening?" questioned a gravelly, querulous voice. It was Olga, a blind lady who had been at the infirmary as long as Didda could remember.

Aunt Thora hurried back to reassure the old woman. The girls could hear their aunt's soothing voice from the next room. Aunt Thora had an easy laughter, great patience, and was the only nurse in the village. She was very striking. Her short black hair had a two-inch wide patch of white above her left eyebrow that went back to just above her left ear. Her right eye was brown and her left eye was blue, like Grand-Amma's eyes. Aunt Thora's husband, Uncle Olaf, was the caretaker of the infirmary. He was a quiet, rather powerfully built man that could, and did, handle any difficult patient. Often, his large brown sweater would droop unevenly below his waist, giving him a bedraggled but comfortable look. His greyish-blond hair was thin and receding although he was not old. He and Aunt Thora were both in their mid-thirties and they loved taking care of people, especially their nieces.

When Aunt Thora returned, she straightened a couple of the pictures and watched as Uncle Olaf settled the girls at the table. As he served them bread and milk they began to calm down.

Aunt Thora stopped fiddling with the pictures, turned, and fixed a sharp stare on Didda. Her black eyebrows pulled together and her mouth pursed in a tight frown, she said grimly, "I want to know about this tröll nonsense." Her chin jutted out as she placed her hand on her hips, glancing at Lilla.

"Didda keeps telling me the trölls are coming, and I'm scared they'll get me." Lilla whimpered.

Crossing her arms, Aunt Thora cocked her head and frowned at Didda. "All right, out with it. Why have you been scaring your sister?"

This was not good; Auntie did not say Diddamin. The Icelandic way of showing fondness was often to add "min", or "mine" to a person's name. Didda opened her mouth just as the chair under her slid. She yelped and jumped toward her aunt, who opened her arms to catch her. "Just a little aftershock, hush now, we're safe."

The house gave another little shudder and a couple of cook pots clattered on the stove. A few glasses clinked in the cabinet. Then, everything quieted down. Thora forgot about being angry as she rocked Didda from side to side while Olaf comforted Lilla.

"Tell me what you have heard about this silly superstition." Aunt Thora said, gently squeezing Didda's shoulders.

"Uncle Bibbi said trölls live in those big black rocks in Vopnafjörður," Didda explained. "He said it was true because there is a recorded history in the Heimskringlan that the trölls first started here. The volcanos opened up with fire and spit them out." Didda shuddered.

"He told me the trölls will come out when an earthquake makes an opening in the cliffs. The trölls will snatch kids, especially the ones that misbehave. They drag them off to be eaten by ogres." Didda buried her face in her aunt's white sweater. She knew she was naughty at times, she was a little stubborn, and sometimes did things she shouldn't. She was sure she would be the first one to be snatched if the trölls came looking.

Didda felt a little shake go through her aunt's body. Was she laughing? Anxiously, Didda peeked at her face. Sure enough, her face puckered up in silent mirth.

"My brother, Bibbi, I should have known." Aunt Thora shook her head. "That is quite a story. Honey, don't you know better than to believe his tall tales? But, you really shouldn't scare your little sister with his stories, or outrageous any ones of your own. I know all about your outrageous imagination." Thora chuckled again.

"You don't believe the trölls are real?" Didda asked, shocked.

"No trolls? The trölls aren't real?" Lilla asked in a squeaky, trembling voice.

"Definitely not real." Olaf said firmly.

Didda got off her aunt's lap. With her hands on her hips, she planted her feet apart and with a pugnacious stare, first at aunt, then at her uncle, demanded, "You don't think the trölls are real?"

Didda was sure such heresy would bring the wrath of the trölls upon all of them! "What about the monster-worm? Everyone knows he is real and lives in the lake not far from the mountains over there." Didda pointed to the mountain range across the fjord. "He is just as bad as the trölls are, causing bad things to happen. I've heard people whisper about that one, Auntie." Didda's voice rose in indignation.

Uncle Olaf buried his face in Lilla's hair, trying to hide his smile as Aunt Thora snorted.

"You silly goose, of course he's not real either." Her aunt was unable to control her laughter. Didda did not like this one bit. She bent forward and looked her aunt straight in the eye, wrinkled her nose, and scrunched her face.

"Well, what about the Hidden People?" Didda did not stamp her foot but sure felt like it. She had learned all about Iceland's history and legends from Uncle Bibbi and could not believe Aunt Thora was sitting there saying the stories were not real.

Uncle Bibbi's story time was legendary. Didda enjoyed the delicious thrill of fear that crawled up her spine, as Bibbi would drop his voice to a whisper. "Hush, listen, don't you hear the moaning and the wailing?" He would say. Then, curling his fingers into claws, he would suddenly grab her and make her screech with fright.

Then he would become serious. "Do not wander too far away from the ruts the cows and horses have made, Diddamin. The animals know their way, but it is easy for folks to get lost out there. When a thick fog comes up suddenly, and that happens so often here in our fjord, I let Thunder take over and guide me home. Always remember, if ever you find yourself lost, let your horse, the dog, or even the old cow, Red, guide you. Take a hold of a tail and don't let go." Bibbi was eighteen and, in between unmerciful teasing, he did teach her quite a bit about safety in their remote country.

Seeing Didda's posture, Thora stopped laughing. Looking sideways at Olaf, she gnawed at her lower lip as she reached out her hand to the young girl.

"I'm sorry, Diddamin. I should not laugh. You are right. Some things cannot be explained, but you can be sure trölls and monsters are not real and you don't have to be afraid of them. People that believe in "Hidden Folks" say that they are kind, and helpful. And there are many tales about those beings, how they have guided folks to safety after they had lost their way on fog-shrouded tundra." Thora paused a moment, then with a serious look she continued. "I have no personal experience with the Hidden, but I do believe in being kind to strangers. Now, what story did you tell Lilla that scared her so?"

"If I tell the story now, won't Lilla start screaming? She always screams." Didda bumped into the stove as she backed away from her aunt.

As if to prove her right, Lilla let out a blood-curdling howl when the big black kettle careened off the stove and crashed noisily to the floor, the lid banging away as it rolled into a corner of the kitchen and came to a quivering stop. None of them had noticed how precariously close the pot was to the edge. Fortunately, it was empty. Thora sighed as she picked up the pot and lid and placed them back on top of the stove. There were no more tremors and no aftershocks.

"Let's sit outside for a while and you can tell me the stories your uncle has been feeding you. Olaf and Lilla can take some coffee to Olga."

They walked down a short path and seated themselves on a flat lava rock. The northern breeze blowing across ocean was chilly even though it was June. They each had on warm Icelandic knit sweaters.

Taking Didda's right hand, her aunt rubbed it with both of hers.

"I'm not angry with you, Diddamin. Well, I was just a little bit angry at first. It is just that I do not want you and Lilla to be scared of these folktales. That is all they are, you know. "

"But I've read many stories from the books in Grandpa's attic, and I asked Bibbi about them." Didda argued. "He said they were all true." She was not about to give up her favorite daydreams.

"So what makes Lilla so very scared?" Her aunt narrowed her left blue eye almost shut.

Rubbing the toe of her right sheepskin shoe into the dirt, Didda drew little circles, giving her aunt a sideways, sheepish look.

"I told her that the trölls are full of tricks and always cause trouble." Didda admitted. "The Hidden Folks are kind and try to help when the trölls have been mean. I was a little scared when Uncle Bibbi said the trölls snatch naughty little kids. I told Lilla since she was the littlest, she would be the easiest one to catch so, she'd better be good or she'd be snatched for sure. "

Thora got up, brushing her skirt. "Well, it's not nice of you to scare her like that. You should be taking care of your pretty little sister."

Ah, there it is, Didda though. People often spoke of Lilla as the 'pretty little girl', which meant she was the most lady-like. Sissi had 'a head on her shoulders' which meant she was the smart one, while Didda, she was a tomboy. That usually meant 'one of these days she's going to break her fool-hardy neck'. Didda loved her two sisters, but she did not like to be the one in the middle - not the younger, pretty one, and not the older, smart one, just the average one in the middle.

"Is that all? Did you tell her anything else you want to share?" Aunt Thora asked.

"Well, I did tell her if we stare hard into the fog, or clouds, or the cliffs, we might see the faces of trölls and ghosts." The loose scoria from the tremor rolled and crunched under Didda's feet as she walked over to the cliff that sheltered the house.

"Can't you see this face over here, Aunt?" Timidly, Didda pointed to two black holes in a crag in the lava-rock wall. "See? Two eyes, a long curvy nose, and an open mouth with long whiskers on a huge chin. Why is it we so often hear that awful wailing and moaning all around us if it's not ghosts and not the naughty children the trölls have taken? "

"Now you've added ghosts? You are hopeless! " Her aunt plunked back down shaking her head. "First, that is not a face, just a formation from an old lava flow. Fog and clouds will do similar formations. Some people say they can see a man's face in a full moon. It is all in the imagination, and you have more than your share of that! " She chuckled. "As far as the moaning noise is concerned, that is just the wind. You know that here, the wind constantly blows through all the crooks and crannies of the volcanic cliffs. They do make odd sounds, especially when it's the northern wind."

Didda was not finished. "Why do all the places have names? The farms, the mountains, the waterfalls? "

Thora turned and stared at Didda for a second, shaking her head in an 'I-give-up' gesture. After a moment, she said, "Folks have been giving names to places forever, something that has a meaning for them or a description."

"Well then," Didda argued. "If there are no trolls, why name a

waterfall Trollfoss, or name a lake Tröll Lake, or Tröll Peninsula, or...
" Her aunt gave her a scorching look that told Didda she had gone
too far. She clamped her mouth shut, but inside she felt giddy with
triumph. There were trolls, she knew it!

Abruptly, Thora got up, smoothing her hand over her backside,
and started for the house. Her skirt swished and billowed as her long
legs strode firmly up the walk.

Didda followed with somewhat subdued elation. As they entered
the house, her aunt turned and gave her "the look." Didda knew she
had better drop the subject. Aunt Thora and Mother had this similar
approach to correcting behavior. They did not use angry words, or
spankings, just what Sissi, Lilla and Didda called *The Look*. Frankly,
there were many times Didda would rather have had the spanking
than the guilty feeling she got from *The Look*.

Uncle Olaf and Lilla had been busy. Soup bowls and coffee cups
were on the table along with a couple of glasses of milk for the girls.
Didda thanked her uncle and took a sip, then cocked her head as the
lively music from old Olga's harmonica drifted into the kitchen. Olga
might be old and blind, and at times exceedingly cranky, but she sure
could belt out the music! Didda envied the old woman's ability. When
Uncle Bibbi tried to teach her the harmonica, Didda tried unsuccess-
fully to imitate the old woman's style. She found she did better with
the accordion, but was not very good at that either.

Her uncle left the kitchen, and Didda heard the music stop. Olga
came into the kitchen shuffling her feet across the floor, guided by
Olaf. Her white hair was tucked up into a green nightcap that folded
over the left side of her face. The long white tassel on the end flopped
in her eyes as she sank heavily into her chair. Wiggling and sighing,
she tucked her ample skirt under her thick thighs.

"Your Grandpa will be here pretty soon to pick you up, Diddamin." Aunt Thora said as she dished up mutton soup. "He'll want to
load up his supplies and head home right away so he won't miss the
tide." Turning, she looked at Didda and asked, "Do you have your
bags ready?"

Didda nodded, knowing that missing the outgoing tide would
add hours to their travel time to the farm, since they would have to
skirt around the inlet instead of across it to get to the other side. Lilla

and Didda stayed with their aunt for three weeks while Sissi had gone directly to Grandpa's farm. Didda was now old enough to help with haying and other chores.

They had just started the meal when there was a commotion outside. The sound of horses snorting and trotting horses and jangling of harnesses was met with old Snati's an enthusiastic barking. Blackie, Grandpa's dog, responded with equal enthusiasm.

Two adults and two children tore out of the house at a dead run. Didda leaped into her Grandpa's arms as Lilla wrapped her arms around his right leg. Thora and Olaf were hugging Sissi. All six of them talking and laughing at the same time.

After they secured the four horses to the weather-beaten wood post, they all went inside, arm-in-arm. Grandpa and Sissi slid into chairs at the table. Olaf walked across the kitchen and took down extra cups and saucers. Placing them up on the table, he poured coffee into each, and then sat down. Thora dipped up soup for her father and Sissi.

As she handed him the brimming bowl, Thora asked. "Did the tremor do any damage at the farm, Dad?"

"No, not at our place," he said. "The livestock in the sheepcote got a little nervous, but then they enjoyed the unexpected shower of hay that tumbled down from the loft." Grandpa held his beard back with his left hand as he blew on his hot soup. Grandpa had very thick, black hair now peppered with gray. Bushy eyebrows over keen, dark-brown eyes and a handlebar, greying mustache that he had a habit of twirling when meditating, or working on endless math-problems.

"I did see where snow slithered down in the clefts between the high crags further inland. We do not have anything to worry about." His bright-blue eyes twinkled as he looked at the two girls. "Just a little greeting from our peculiar country."

Thora turned with a raised eyebrow and looked at Didda as if to say, "See I told you so!"

CHAPTER 2

On the Way to Grandpa's Farm

As they came to the top of the moss and lichen covered lava ridge, Didda could see that the tide was way out. Grandpa's timing was perfect. He guided the horse, Patches, into the deep hoof-ruts carved out by many years of use. The three packhorses followed, two carrying the girls, Didda on one and Sissi on the other. The third was a young colt that carried Didda's suitcase and a food satchel. Their grandfather allowed only a light burden on the young horse while training him.

The sure-footed Icelandic horses trod down the lava rock riddled hill with ease; even the two of them carried the extra weight of the children. The loads were well balanced, with each of the girls positioned squarely in the middle, wedged between the two packsaddle pommels. The easy gaits of the horses made the ride akin to sitting in a rocking chair, except swaying side to side instead of back and forth, Didda mused as she enjoyed the sensation.

They stopped at the edge of the ocean inlet. Patches snorted and pulled towards a small, gurgling creek that tumbled down the hillside and into the shallow, salty bay. With one easy movement, Grandpa was out of the saddle and led his horse to the water, then came over and lifted each of the girls off their horses.

Didda watched as her grandfather checked the girths, harnesses, and baggage, giving an extra yank on the oilskin covering the flour and sugar. As she stood by her horse, Rusty, she stared across the bay. The horses were enjoying the short break and started nibbling on the sparse, pale-green grass. Sissi's horse, Star, and the colt, Pretty, had finished slurping noisily in the ice-cold creek. A flock of geese darted off in a flutter of feathers, while the gannets haughtily stuck their long, pointy bills into the air, then flew up and came after them, angry at being disturbed. By beating the air with their horses' whips and yelling back at their screeching, they fought the birds off.

"Grandpa, why didn't you come after me in your boat this time?" Didda asked. She had thought he preferred to use his fishing to travel across the bay to the village, Vopnafjörður (wop-na-f'yore dur) where her aunt and uncle lived.

"The motor has been acting up. I've got it torn apart to clean. I'll have it ready for the next trip in." Her grandpa replied.

"Well, I can clean it for you. You have showed me how to do that!" Didda grinned.

"I'm sure you could." He chuckled as he shaded his eyes against the misty sun, dimly glittering through low-lying clouds over the dark, distant hills. Rubbing his grey-whiskered chin, his eyes scoured the seashore across the bay. Then chuckling, he pointed to the mouth of the inlet where the surface quivered and rippled. Sisi and Didda held their breath as five little brown heads popped up. Ten large shining black eyes inspected the intruders with curiosity. The baby seals were totally unafraid. The two girls were fascinated as they watched the babies playfully swim, diving up and down, barking noisily, until older seals showed up and shooed them out to the open ocean.

"Those Harbor Seals know the tide is about to turn. We'd better go across now." Their grandfather swung into the stirrups of his saddle and whistled for Blackie. Patting the rump of his horse, he motioned to his dog. "Come up here, Old Man." Didda watched as the stirrups skimmed the ocean water that came up to the horses' knees, thinking how small the Icelandic horses were. Some polar bears are bigger than they are.

Turning in his saddle grandfather looked at the girls. "Hold unto the pommels with both hands but give the horse a free rein," he said. "The horses are quite used to this path, but the ocean floor can change with every earth tremor, even a small one like we just had. It can leave pockets of holes. If Rusty or Star stop, do not urge them. Just wait and let them decide if it is safe to go on. I'll be watching." Sissi and Didda somberly nodded as he patted the neck of his horse and continued across.

Didda peered into the water, while her sister warily eyed her with Aunt Thora's don't-you-dare look. Grinning impishly, Didda whispered, "If you look real close, Sissi, there's some kind of gruesome, greenish tail right by Star's right hoof!" She made a big show of squinting her eyes as she looked down.

"If there were, Star would stop," Sissi hissed. "You can scare Lilla, but not me."

Didda would have been better off paying attention to her horse who kept swishing and lifting his tail, his rump giving off loud rumbling noises. Then Rusty stopped, the other horses kept going. Slowly, Didda became aware that she wasn't sitting upright. She was leaning precariously to the left, her body slowly inching down until her long braids brushed the water. Just as she opened her mouth to yell, Rusty shifted his body and Didda found herself underwater. She gulped and ended up with mouthful of salty water.

"Grandpa, Rusty's girth is loose and Didda is drowning!" Sissi shrieked at the top of her lungs. The next thing Didda knew, Grandpa's strong arms lifted her up. He placed her up on Pretty's back, then handing her his red bandana, reeking of tobacco, to dry her face. She gagged on the water, spluttered and spit. She felt chastened - she should have known better than to joke about a water-monster!

"What's the matter, boy?" Grandfather ran his hand over Rusty's flank. "Ah, gas" Tightening the girth again, he lifted Didda off Pretty.

"You'll be all right now on Rusty, Diddamin. Pretty has all she can carry." Didda nodded, she knew her grandfather was very protective of his horses and took exceedingly good care of them He liked to wait until the colts were four to five years old before breaking them to saddle.

When they were halfway across the inlet, the first wave rolled in, almost imperceptibly. Soon, the water was lapping at the bellies of the horses. When they reached the shore, they quickly scrambled up the black volcanic sand littered with slimy kelp and brown seaweed. Their hoofs slid as they worked their way between wet, barnacle-riddled lava rocks until they reached the mossy bank. Following the rut, they reached a slight hill where they dismounted.

Blackie took off like an arrow shot from a bow. A riotous squawking and the whirring of wings disturbed the quiet countryside as a flock of rjúpa flew from the hollows of the moss-covered basalt rocks. Blackie came back with a self-satisfied look on his old face. His mouth was open; his long tongue flopped as he mightily shook his body.

He looked like he was laughing his head off, Didda thought. She had asked how old he was. No one could agree what his age was, but she thought he might be as old as Grandpa. They both had grey whiskers.

Blackie was a superb livestock herder. And, according to Grandpa, no dog in any of the nearby farms was as good as he in herding the sheep during réttir. The réttir - roundup – was a festive in the fall celebrated by the farmers after they separated and claimed their sheep according to their markings. Blackie was relentless and did not seem to care how far he had to go. Grandpa truly had bragging rights when it came to his dog, a powerfully built animal with a thick, shiny coat, mostly black in color. His four paws were brown-tipped as were his long, straight ears. He had a tuft of brown on the very tip of his tail.

While Blackie was lapping at a small pond, fed by a short tumbling waterfall, and the horses nibbled on grass tufts. The girls sat cross-legged on the soft grey moss, while their Grandpa perched on a large lava boulder. Didda ran her hand over a small berry-patch, but it was too early in the season. The blueberries were green, rock-hard nubs, just barely starting to grow. It will be August before we get to taste them, Didda sighed.

Then she watched her Grandpa opening a brown burlap sack. Digging into the bag, he came up with sandwiches of dark rye bread heavily smeared with butter with thick slices of cheese. Pulling out a long piece of dried cod, he peeled off strips and handed some to each girl. Then, as a dessert, each one got two twist cookies. They ate contently for a while, watching the inlet fill up as the tide swept in. The silvery bodies of salmon and trout shot up into the air and dropped back into the water with soft, plopping sounds. Rings formed on the water and floated to the shores in ever widening, diminishing circles.

A seagull winged her way down and landed on a small patch of black sand, cocking her head first to one side then the other. She studied Didda for a moment with her beady eyes, and then swiftly took off toward Didda. *I can just read her tiny mind, she is after my cookies!* Didda jumped up and shooed the bird away amid the screaming of other greedy gulls that now had gathered to grab their share. One headed for Sisi.

Didda yelled, "Get her Sissi - get her."

"How do you know it's a 'her'?" Grandpa roared with laughter as he, too, was fighting off the crazy birds.

"This bird just looked smaller than the others and just looked like a lady bird but sure didn't act like one." Didda huffed, out of breath as they gathered the food left over from their meal. A thick band of fog was rolling in from the mouth of the fjord. The sounds of motors starting up from two fishing boats caused them to pause and watch as they headed toward Vopnafjörður harbor.

"Well." Grandpa drawled. "Looks like we got across just in time. From the looks of that fog, we may be in for a soupy time. We'd better get a move on."

After washing down their food with a cool drink from the little waterfall, they remounted. With Patches leading, they continued in the hoof-ruts that were so deep in places that their grandfather's feet were literally dragging on the ground. He lifted his feet and spread them out wide as he came to higher mounds of moss and grass-covered rocks. Didda's horse was at the end of the caravan.

The days were getting longer and there would be no real darkness from now until fall. The nights would get lighter and lighter until the sun would dangle on the horizon all night. Now, only a dusky, grey sky gave an eerie look to the black, craggy cliffs. A small farmstead sat far back in the hills, barely discernable in the gravelly background. Streams wandered and gurgled down in small waterfalls then disappeared into gravelly beds. The countryside was bleak and sparse. Meager grass-tufts were sprinkled with patches of purple wildflowers, which somehow were able grow roots between the moss and lichen.

The waves of white fog were wallowing in like a slow-moving avalanche when Grandpa held his right hand up, indicating that they should stop. He then took a rope from his saddlebag and rode in front of Socks. Tying the rope to the pommel in front of Sissi he then proceeded to tie Pretty. Rusty was next. Then he guided Patches to the back holding the rope loosely in his hand as he motioned to Sissi.

"Sissi, Star will now lead," he said. "The fog may get so thick we'll not be able to see one another. I want to be sure we won't get separated." Sissi nodded as she moved her horse to the front of their caravan.

Well, for once, Didda was happy to be the middle child. She thought the oozing, slithering fog in the fjord was the creepiest thing.

It seemed to her that the whole countryside became a very different world, filled with ghostly cities and Hidden People constantly moving and changing shapes. At the same time, she was fascinated by the strangeness of the grey-white rolling mist that never looked the same. The sure-footed horses plodded along, staying in the deep path. They did not hesitate or stumble, even when the fog caught up with them and the rut totally disappeared from sight.

In no time, it was as if they had been covered with a huge, silver-grey downy duvet. The swirling damp fog was tangible, filling Didda's mouth and nose. She thought she could take a handful and wad it up like a snowball. She could no longer see Sissi, and Pretty was a moving grey blur. She turned and looked behind her; Grandpa was a hunched-down shadowy shroud, rocking side to side.

Then came the welcoming sounds of hoofs clomping on the wooden bridge that spanned a small glacial-fed creek which swiftly rushed by their Grandpa's farm. Suddenly, there was a small rift in the fog, as if someone had flung back gauzy curtains. A slight wind had come up and slowly the fog dissipated in twists, swirls and spirals. The path widened, flattened and became more visible.

"We are here, we made it!" Sissi yelled eagerly. She had spotted the open gate with the metal arch etched with the name of the farm, Hamundarstaðir, (Ha-mun-dar-sta-thur) in bold letters. The loaded-down horses picked up their pace and trotted up to the front door that was flung open by Bibbi, followed by Grandma Sigga and Great-Grandma close at his heels.

Grandfather's farmhouse was a complex of three wood-gable fronts, built side by side and divided by two short walls of rock and turf. The roof and each end of the gables were covered with turf that grew thick, green grass where the girls constantly had to chase off the sheep. This type of farmhouse was called Gable Farm. In the middle gable was the main entrance to the hall, the passageway to the kitchen, and the stairs to Grandpa's attic room.

The left-side wall of the dark, hard-packed dirt floor was finished with rough, wooden boards. Several wood pegs were placed at various heights for men's, women's and children's coats. There were also pegs for the horsewhips everyone owned; lightweight, heavyweight, short, long. Some plain and some very elegantly silver adorned, handsomely carved with the initial of the owner. An assortment of bridles hung on heavy, higher-up pegs. The right side of the hall had a wall of various size stone and daubed with solidly packed dirt, and a door leading to the cow-house. Very convenient for milking in the winter.

A narrow dung trough went across the entire width and to the opposite wall. About a foot up this wall was a two-foot square opening with a hinged door. On the other side was a huge hole where Bibbi pitched the manure, which in time disappeared in the porous volcanic ground.

This was also the bathroom when it was too cold to go outside to the outhouse. When Didda had to squat over the dung-trough, to use the facility. She had to be sure to hold a cow's tail or she would get a whopping slap. Just outside the front door was the hitching post where folks would tie the horses' reins. A weather vane sat on top of the central gable. The small outhouse nearby was also covered with turf, except for the front where the wood door with the half-moon was.

Bibbi lifted Sissi off the packsaddle as Grandpa came around to Rusty. Swinging Didda down and holding her in his arms as if she were a baby, he handed her to Grandma, who promptly started kissing and hugging her. Sissi stood by, grinning from ear-to-ear. Didda could tell by the gleeful look on Sissi's face that she was just dying to tell Grandma how she had saved Didda's life. She would probably tell how Didda had been teasing her about the monster-worm. Didda glanced sideways at her sister. She looked like the cat that swallowed the whole bird, as Grandma would say. Didda would have to come up with something mighty quick to stop her.

"It is wonderful to see you, Diddamín." Grand-Amma got up from her rocking chair shooing the plump black cat off her lap. Gryla yowled and took off, swishing her tail with displeasure. The cat ran over and rubbed against Didda's ankles as Grand-Amma gave her great granddaughter a hug. With an arm resting on Didda's shoulder, Grand-Amma turned to Sissi.

"Pour us some coffee, my love, and let Didda tell me all about your Aunt Thora and your trip," she said. "I was really getting concerned when the fog rolled in so quickly." Their Grand-Amma sat back down with a deep sigh. She was rather plump and was often short of breath.

Didda helped Sissi get the cups and saucers off the wooden shelf. They settled themselves in the kitchen where the scent of boiling coffee and soup blended in a delicious aroma that permeating the air. The girls watched as Grandma cut slices of hot bread and spread on a thick layer of butter. Didda's stomach growled so loud that Grandma exclaimed, "Are you starving? Didn't that man feed you?" She glared at their Grandfather who was coming through the door, slapping and rubbing his cold hands together.

"Oh yes, Grandma, Grandpa fed us," Sissi and Didda eagerly spoke up at the same time.

"It just smells so good in here that my stomach got greedy." Didda jumped up and grabbed her grandma around the neck. "I am so very happy to be here. I liked it at Aunt Thora's house too, but I really missed all of you and missed doing things with Sissi." Didda snuck a look at her sister, thinking the compliment might make Sissi go easy on her.

"Oh, it will be fun to have you here. We'll go egg hunting and berry-picking, milk Old Red..." She said, then stopped and gave Didda a big grin. Was her sister being her nice self, or was there a wicked gleam in her eyes as she mentioned the milking? Didda was sure that Grandpa's Old Red was the meanest cow in all of Iceland.

Later, laying in the dark she listened to the wind blowing outside. She mused about the monster-worm, the trölls and the hidden people. The creaks and groans of the old farmhouse would have been scary if not for the pure enjoyment of being here.

Didda wiggled contently into the downy duvet just as Gryla jumped onto the bed and lay next to her. She slept - one hand on Gryla's soft paws.

CHAPTER 3

Old Red (Gamla Rauða)

Sissi and Didda entered the cow house, the chickens fussed and the vicious threatening rooster cackled. Each time Didda stuck her hand into a nest to gather eggs, he would spread out his red-gold wings, screech, and glare at her with his glittering tiger-yellow eyes.

One of these days, grandma will get tired of you attacking her and us. She will wring your scrawny neck and you will end up in her stew-pot, Didda thought. She glared at the rooster she backed away and joined Sissi. They walked over to the cow-stall, Didda holding on to the milk-bucket with her right hand, and her sister with her left.

Didda tiptoed away from Sissi, carefully sidestepping Old Red's droppings. She grabbed a three-legged wooden milk-stool with both hands. Clutching the stool, Didda tried not to breathe the potent dung smell.

Sissi swept a squawking chicken off the closest cow's back and took the stool out of Didda's hand. She stomped ahead of Didda to the infamous old cow's stall.

"Now hold unto Old Red's tail, don't let her whack me!" Sissi demanded.

Sissi detested milking the cows, detested going into the reeking stalls, and especially detested Old Red, who either slapped them with her gross tail or slathered them with the gross, slimy yuck from her long tongue. The nasty-tempered cow would kick the girls' legs or the milk bucket at every opportunity. She was forever butting her horns into the wall and had dug out a huge hole. Didda thought for sure one day the cow would bore an opening right through the thick dirt wall. Old Red was one crabby old cow.

"Why don't you tie her tail to her leg?" Didda grumbled. "That's what Grandma does." Didda did not like this chore either.

Sissi glared at her sister. "No, just hold the tail" Didda did her best. Her arm flew from side to side, trying to hold on as the cow flipped her tail, trying just as hard to free it from Didda's grip. Didda grit her teeth as he held on. "I would have tied the yucky thing."

Sissi did a good job. The spurts of milk made pinging sounds as they hit the insides of the pail, the milky froth piling up. Old Red was a mean-spirited cow but she gave lots of good milk, with very thick cream. Her udder was full and tight with milk. Didda thought the cow must be quite uncomfortable, as the animal seemed rather subdued for a change.

After the milking, Sissi stood up and placed the pail in the corner by the door. Didda let go of the tail and, Old Red, relieved of the weight on her udder, predictably kicked back and sent the stool flying into the side of Freyja, the heifer in the next stall. The subsequent out-of-control bedlam was stupefying - cows bellowing, chickens squawking, the girls screaming wildly and jumping, trying to get out of the way of flailing tails. There was not a whole lot of room for them to duck.

"Stupid, dumb cow," Didda howled as Old Red's tail swatted her across the back.

"What in heavens name is going on?" Grandma came running into the cow-house.

"Old Red got mad at me for holding her tail." Didda was steamed.

"Well, she is used to her tail being tied. Try that the next time you milk her." Grandma shook her head as she picked up the milk bucket and went back into the kitchen.

Glancing at her sister Didda tried to give her Aunt Thora's "I told you so" look. It did not do her any good because Sissi completely ignored her as they followed their grandmother into the house. They sat contentedly and watched as she poured the milk into the two-spout separator. Grand-Amma was sitting on a stool, her left hand on the handle ready to crank the machine. It was not long before the thick cream came out of one spout while the thinner milk gushed out of the other. G   Grandma poured the cream into a wood churn, and then Didda and Sissi took turns slushing the butter-paddle up and down, until they heard the solid mass of butter plopping at the bottom. Grandma reached down into the churn, took out the big blob of butter, and salted it. Setting the butter aside, Grandma turned to the oven and pulled out two loaves of bread.

The mouth-watering aroma of the fresh-baked bread permeated the kitchen. It missed with smell of the constantly cooking mutton soup that simmered away all day. Grand-Amma pulled the bread out of the oven and set it beside the always-full coffeepot. Didda sniffed deeply, devouring the delicious bouquet mix.

Slicing the hot bread, Grandma put on a thick slab of butter before handing each girl a slice. The melting butter ran between their fingers and they licked as fast as they could, Sissi licking ever so daintily as Didda slurped noisly.

Grandma picked up the pail containing the thinner skimmed milk and walked over to the storage area of the kitchen. She poured the milk into a short wooden tub. Next to the milk tub sat the tubs for the pickled herring, pickled whale blubber and the singed-and-pickled sheep heads - eyeballs intact - all preserved and stored in wooden barrels.

A side of smoked mutton and dried cod hung from a rack above the barrels. Didda liked the dried cod very much and could nibble on all day. The storage area also held fermented shark, which neither Didda nor Sissi liked at all.

Grandma added a small lump of skyr into the skimmed-milk tub. Skyr was Icelandic yogurt. This clump would start the setting process for a new batch. She would always save a handful from one batch to be added to the next. This method of making skyr started with the Vikings. For centuries since, a small amount was saved from one batch to the next to continue the fermenting process.

The next day, the family would have more of the yummy skyr for breakfast, served with cream and sugar sprinkled on top. Later in the summer, they would top it with blueberries, when the berries were ripe.

CHAPTER 4

Haying Time

"I have lunch ready and need both of you need to go out to the field to take food to your Grandpa and the workers." Grandma said as she turned to Didda. "Diddamin, Star and Rusty are just outside the fence. Go and get them while Sissi helps me to finish up here."

Grand-Amma, who had been watching Grandma as she bustled about, arose from her chair with a deep sigh and followed Didda out of the kitchen.

"I guess you both are riding bareback as usual?" She asked in somewhat disapproving tone. "The way you two gallivant on those horses is not very lady-like." Shaking her head, she reached up with a blue-veined hand to one of the top pegs and took down two bridles. Didda grinned as she took the harnesses out of her hand. Both girls knew that Grand-Amma thought the only way for a lady to ride a horse was side-saddle, in a split-style skirt.

"Thanks, Grand-Amma. You are right; Sissi and I won't be bothering with saddles." Giving her a quick peck on the cheek Didda darted out the door and jogged across the field. The bridles clunked on her shoulders as she leaped between moss-covered lava rocks. Hearing the noise, Rusty and Star lifted their head where they had been nibbling on the meager, pale-green tufts of grass. Neighing and snorting, they ambled toward Didda.

Pretty came running and nuzzled against her. Didda liked her and thought she was growing up to be very special. She had a shiny, silver-grey coat with a coal-black mane and tail. Her eyes were large, bright and intelligent. Didda rubbed behind Pretty's left ear. She seemed to sense Didda's affection and whinnied softly.

"Sorry girl, you stay put." Didda patted the velvet-soft nose.

Star and Rusty trotted up as Didda rattled the reins. She slid a bit in Star's mouth, then one into Rusty's. She gave Pretty couple of sugar cubes before swatting her on the rump, and watched as the colt scampered away.

Star was a reliable grey mare, with long white mane and tail. Rusty was a glistening-red color with a narrow white narrow stripe from her eyes to her nostrils, and white socks on all four feet. They all held their head proudly, a sure sign of loved and well-tended horses.

Stepping up on top of a tall stone, Didda jumped on Rusty's back, and holding Star's rein, galloped back to the farmhouse.

Grand-Amma, Grandma, and Sissi were all outside waiting. Didda did not dismount since the food was all packed and ready. Sissi put her left foot on the hitching-rock, and swung her right foot over Star's back and wiggled a bit, as she settled herself. Each of them had food satchels and milk pails in front of them. They waved as they headed for the valley where Grandpa, uncle Bibbi, and the summer help, Helgi, Gunna and Disa were cutting and drying hay. Grass grew sparsely around the farm and Grandpa had to go way up into the foothills of the mountains to find enough to cut and store away for the winter.

They went at an easy canter past the stable, down the lane and over the bridge. As soon as they crossed the bridge, the horses went swiftly into rack, and then into the flying pace, a five-gait that is unique to Icelandic horses. Bibbi liked to show off the smooth gait by carrying a glass of water and riding his horse, Thunder, at break-neck without spilling a single drop.

Rusty and Star kept up the galloping run across the outer field until they reached the start of the foothills. They heard Patches whinny before they saw him. Rusty and Star neighed back. Biting their bits, they eagerly plunged up the hill. The path led to an incredible volcanic cliff formation that pointed to the sky filled with mystic shapes and deep crevasses. Didda thought it was the perfect place for Trölls to live. Suddenly, a couple of ptarmigans scrambled away from the hooves of Rusty, startling Didda, but not her tranquil horse.

"Hey, Sissi, you know there are trölls living up there, don't you?" Didda's hands were gripping the reins. Rusty sensed her tension, shaking his head he grunted with displeasure with her and the exertion of going uphill.

Sissi turned, dark brows knit tightly over the bridge of her nose.

"Stop it, Didda. Iceland is weird, and weird things happen, but there are NO TROLLS" She shouted the last words.

Why was she shouting Didda wondered? When did her eleven-and-a-half year old sister get to be so grown up and start sounding like Aunty? Turning away, Didda stared at the high crags where few long wispy fingers of fog were curling over the edges. The cool sun was playing hide and seek in the fluffy cottony clouds, sending eerie grey shadows stealthily moving across the mountain.

Didda turned and looked down toward the ocean. The farm was hard to see unless you knew where to look - the turf roof blended with the ground. The house looked like a toy house in the distance, sitting precipitously at the very edge on the cliff that skirted the long fjord.

The horses clambered over the last hill, and there were the workers. Grandpa's scythe was swinging up and down, Helgi was a few feet behind him and Bibbi was a few feet behind Helgi. Each man had a firm grip on the two knobby handles on the long pole, swinging their scythes in perfect rhythm. Up-down-swish-up-down-swish. The curve of the sharp blades smoothly cutting the grass. The two women followed behind raking the green newly cut leaves into rows of long narrow piles. Four bales of hay were tied up and ready to be taken to the farm.

"Lunchtime," Sissi and Didda hollered unnecessarily as the workers were already laying down their tools. The rare sun had made all of them work up a sweat, their knit sweaters were piled up on a large lava rock.

The men pulled out their fancy tobacco-horns. Grandpa's was by far the most ornate. He and Bibbi poured snuff on the back of their left hand while Helgi poured his on the back of his right hand. Snuffing mightily, each sat down on a moss-covered rock.

Gunna handed the bags to Disa who started passing the food around. The two women, both in their twenties, were as different as night and day. Blond-haired Gunna was short and slim with sky-blue twinkling eyes. Merry, easy-going and given to teasing, she and Bibbi got along extremely well. She was also a whirlwind of a worker that Grandpa really appreciated. Disa, on the other hand, had red hair and temper to go with it. She was tall and graceful, striking-looking with green eyes. She also pulled no punches when it came to work.

Helgi was a quiet, thirty-something, brown haired, square-built man. Well known for his strength, he was an undefeated arm-wrestler in the area. Even though there was such an age difference, he and Bibbi got along well. Eighteen-year old Bibbi had an outgoing nature and was very popular with the young folks as he played his accordion at many country-dances in the village.

After lunch was finished, they put everything away and went back to work, with Sissi and Didda joining the crew. They worked together for several hours.

The men cut grass steadily, occasionally stopping to sharpen their scythes. They would pull out a pumice stone from their back pocket, spit on the scythe blades, and then swish the stone back and forth. They started at the pole and following the curve of the blade to the end of the point. Periodically, with a thumb, they would check the blade until satisfied with its sharpness.

Gunna and Disa followed, raking and turning the rows of grass that smelled faintly of thyme and crowberry leaves. Sissi and Didda worked with Gunn and Disa, doing their best to keep up. Sissi did a good job and seemed to be able to keep focused on the work. Didda tended to stop and breathe in the aroma of the cut grass, look around, and frequently inspect the odd-looking, black lava cliff.

Leaning on her rake, Didda wiped the sweat off her face with the back of her hand, staring for a minute at the rocky crags before turning back to raking. A short time later, she looked where they had been working. None of the rows was straight for any length. There were several outcroppings of rock scattered about and they had to cut the grasses around them. Didda hoped they were not disturbing the Hidden Folks that live in those rocks. At least they were not moving any of the rocks. She had heard that sometimes farmers moved rocks to clear a field and nothing but grief came from it. Didda heard the stories of missing tools, broken equipment, sickness among the animals and all sorts of trouble. Icelanders learned very quickly never to disrupt a rock that could be home to the Hidden. Sometimes even roads went around a rock rather than move it.

Lost in her daydreaming, Didda dropped her rake. It clattered noisily against one of the boulders. Shivering and mumbling an apology, she started raking like one possessed. Sissi turned at the noise.

"Wow, you got pumped up all of a sudden." She grinned. She sure has a way of reading my mind, chewing on her bottom lib Didda glared at her sister, then turned and concentrated on her raking.

The crimson-streaked clouds brushed the tops of the cliffs and hid the sun as it dangled in the northern sky. To the east, the clouds on the horizon touched the mouth of the fjord. Sky and sea were turning dark-grey and, as so often in the fjords, it was hard to tell where one started and the other ended.

The wind was picking up and it was getting chilly. The girls and the workers put their sweaters back on and prepared to quit for the day and head back to the farm.

Grandpa got one of the horses and fastened a packsaddle on its back. He hoisted one of the bales of hay and hooked it on the right-side peg. Then he motioned for Didda to do her job. She knew what to do – bending over, she backed her butt up against the flank of the horse and under the bale, holding it up while Grandpa went around and lifted another bale onto the left-side peg. Bibbi put a packsaddle on another horse and lifted up a bale of hay. Sissi held it up in the same manner as Didda had for Grandpa, as the other bale was put into place.

Helgi, Gunna and Disa got the rest of their horses and their caravan started for home. Didda could never figure out how her grandfather could get those bales so perfectly balanced. He had no scales to weigh them. She thought her grandpa was a very smart man.

CHAPTER 5

Egg Gathering

Sitting on the soft, grey, moss-covered volcanic cliff, Didda and Sissi dangled their legs over the edge, watching the white-crested ocean waves roll in. Two screeching seagulls circled, then dove at their head. They flew off when the girls stood up waving their hands, shooing the birds away.

Didda could feel the shaking of the ground as powerful ocean waves crashed against the sea-stacks and sent columns of sea-spray shooting into the air. Fine salty mist clung to her wool cap and moistened her face. For a change, there was not a hint of fog. In the distance across the fjord, a tall white waterfall cascaded down Butter Mountain. Rivers meandered in curvy ribbons down the valley and emptied into the ocean. Big bales of white, cottony clouds filled the ice-blue sky and dialed along in the cool, brisk, steady breeze.

The girls tucked their hair tighter under their wool-caps as they scanned the eider ducks flying about. They watched the ducks land and hoped to see them waddle to a nest among the rocks on the damp lava-sand.

"There are hundreds of ducks. We should be able to get tons of eggs and down." Didda whispered, although they were a good twenty feet above the ocean beach. The insane noise of the gulls and the pounding of the sea would have made it virtually impossible for the ducks to hear her.

"Some of them went into the moss-patch behind the big boulder where that seal is." Sissi pointed. "He will leave when he sees us coming down. Let's go."

She started scrambling down the nearly sheer rock wall. Didda followed close behind. With tiny toeholds and small ledges for their fingers to grip, they crept down slowly. Their progress caused loose shale and lava pebbles to roll. The clatter disturbed some haughty-gaudy puffins that pompously waddled away.

The sisters each had two flour sacks tied to their waist, one for the down and one for the eggs. Didda looked forward to eating those scrumptious eggs. They tasted stronger than chicken eggs and were almost three times larger with a huge reddish-yellow yolk.

The last few feet was loose gravel and sand so they skidded down on their bottoms until they reached the beach. Catching their breath for a moment, they sat still as two groups of grey geese spanned their wings, wide flapped and raucously squawked then went at each other. Didda saw what had them fighting. A large dead trout lay on the ground halfway between the two groups. The birds separated and flew off as the girls got up and started to walk towards the area. Didda was glad those were not gannets, she knew their reputation for attacking with their saber-like pointy beaks.

Sissi was right, the seal belly-flopped off the rock then awkwardly, flip-flopped on the pebbly beach to the ocean where it smoothly swam away.

Finding some nests, the girls gathered two dozen eggs, always leaving one or two in the down filled nests to hatch. They knew that eider ducks rarely lay more than five eggs. After carefully dividing the eggs into two bags and tucking the soft down all around them, they filled the other bags with the downy feathers.

"Grandma will be happy to know that there are so many nests here." Sissi said as she tightened the string on her sack and fastened it back to her waist. "She wants to make more bed-pillows. If it doesn't rain tomorrow, we'll have to get a group of us together and come back." She started to walk back toward the cliff.

"Wait a minute, Sissi. Let's wade for a while." Didda said. "Look, there's a small cave over there. The ocean is so clear I see some pretty neat seashell on the bottom." Didda sat down on a rock and started to take off her shoes, then jumped up howling; "Oh gross, a fulmar has spit his yellow gook here. This rock smells of rotten fish!"

Sissi doubled over with laughter as she unfastened her bags. Turning, she pointed to where they had clawed their way down.

"There are a lot of them nesting in the hollows of the sea-cliff, we are lucky we didn't touch any of their mess. We'd be stinking to high heaven for days." She gave exaggerated shudder. Taking off their shoes and socks, they tiptoed among shells and pebbles. Didda stuck her foot into the pool.

"Wow, the water is ice-cold." She yelped yanking her foot back, shivering. Looking down, she saw small fish darting about. Large, silvery trout swam gracefully in the shallow cave carved out by the unceasing surging of the ocean waves.

Hollering "Ee-ow" at the top of their lungs, they waded in the freezing sea-waves, hopping backward as a wave would roll in and slosh white froth up their legs. The hems of their skirts were getting soaked and it was time to go home. Fastening their bags to their waists, they headed back up the cliff. As they clambered up on all fours, the sandy shale caused their feet to slide one foot back for every two feet upward. Their soggy sheepskin shoes and wool socks were soon caked with powdery, black volcanic sand.

Although the wind was nippy, the girls had beads of sweat on their foreheads by the time they reached the top. They jammed their hats down tighter. The ends of their scarfs whipped across their shoulder and flapped behind them in the strong breeze. Puffing and breathing hard from their climb, they walked and skipped back to the farmhouse. As usual, they had to chase the sheep off the turf roof before going inside.

CHAPTER 6

Didda and Sissi Go Berry-Picking

"The Blueberries should be ripe about now and I would like to have some to make jam, and put on top of our sky." Grandma said as she walked into the kitchen one morning. "How about you two go and pick some, but don't bother to pick any crowberries."

Not waiting for an answer, she reached the bench, and pulled out two tin buckets. Grabbing two folded white flour sacks, she handed on to each of the girls and continued. "The weather looks good today. Your Grandpa and Bibbi have already taken the boat out to the fjord to do some fishing. Disa and Gunna are hoeing the garden." Reaching to the back of the counter, Grandma pulled out two lunch satchels she had prepared earlier. They were bulging and the girls looked at each other happily.

"We'd love to go berry picking," Didda and Sissi cried enthusiastically as they jumped from their stools. They smiled gleefully at each other and had the same thought: riding into the valley, the berry hunting and picking would take most of the day. They would be gone at milking time and would not have to put up with Old Red, the mean old cow.

"Shall we go back to the foothills where we were haying?" Sissi asked casually, reaching around the doorpost and yanking down two rope-bridles.

"The cows meandered over that way, look for them and bring them back with you after you've filled your buckets." Grandma said, grinning. She knew exactly what we had been thinking. Didda squirmed, feeling guilty blush warm her cheeks. Sissi turned with a shrug, wrinkling her nose.

"We'll do that, Grandma." She said, slinging one bridle over her shoulder and handing Didda the other one. Reaching down, she picked up her pail and satchel as Didda picked up hers. The girls kissed Grandma on the cheek and went out the door heading for the field. They waved to Disa who had paused working to wipe sweat off her forehead with white handkerchiefs. The girls called a greeting and Gunna looked up to see their wave. Leaning on the handle of her hoe, she waved back.

Blackie and Goldie got to their feet, stretching. The dainty Goldie lifted up her right paw, grooming it with long strokes by her tongue. Blackie sat up, his dark-brown eyes glittering as he cocked his head.

"Yes, you may go with us." Didda patted his head as his body quivered with excitement. He was probably ten years older than Goldie was, she thought, but still acted and worked like a much younger dog. Didda thought he was ten times smarter than Goldie as well.

Sissi whistled for the horses as the sisters sauntered past the sheepcote. The horses were in the outer field and came trotting toward them. As usual, Didda got Rusty, while Sissi put a bridle on Star. They did not use saddles unless they were visiting other farms. After a brisk one-hour ride, they got close to where they had been haying. The fearsome, grotesquely shaped lava rock loomed forebodingly ahead of them.

Didda could not understand how Sissi could be so calm, almost serene, in these eerie surroundings. Didda loved her rugged, bleak country full of mysteries and adventures, but she also saw ghosts, gremlins and trölls in every crack and crevasse.

They rode past piles of blue-grey lava chunks spaced few meters apart. Travelers from centuries ago had stacked up these landmarks – tall ones and squatty ones – as guideposts. Dotting the valley were towering, skinny, lava-formed pillars with grey-black trunks. Their tops covered with grey velvety moss that grew everywhere. Small, white and purple flowers were somehow able to grab roots in non-existing soil.

After another hour of riding farther into the valley, they spotted the cows ambling away as they munch on the meager grass. A tall waterfall cascaded down the craggy, basalt-formed hill and the wide, shallow river meandered their way. One cow was standing in mid-stream slurping away. This was a good place to stop. The girls led their horses down for a drink then tethered them and went to look for berry-patches. Blackie lapped some water then scampered off to chase birds.

"Kónguló, kónguló, vísaðu mér á berjamó." (Spider, spider show me the berry-patch) they chanted as they searched for ripe, juicy blueberries. Didda and Sissi believed the old folks' stories; the spiders always led the way to the best berry-spots, and they were very careful not to squash those long-legged, helpful creatures.

Sure enough, they came upon a nice area thick with berries. It was getting close to lunchtime so they decided to eat before picking the fruit. Grandma had fixed enough for a small army; strips of dried cod, slices of smoked mutton, and twist cookies. They drank fresh water from the river then started gathering berries. At first Didda could hear them go clunk into the pails, but as the berries accumulated the only sound was a soft plop.

The narrow valley was quiet. Every now and then, a ptarmigan would cluck and dart out from under a small bush, wings whirring. The horses occasionally snorted softly, and the cows chewed contently. The air was calm. A faint, salty smell from the ocean mingled with thyme and berries. A few fluffy clouds wandered across the sharp-blue sky.

Sissi had crawled up the hillside and was furiously picking away. She bent the branches down with her left hand, and busily picked off the berries with her right. Didda's bucket was over half-full, but the way her sister was going, Didda was sure she had her bucket almost full. Didda sat back on her heels and glanced at the craggy mountain. Then did a double take. Thick fog was gathering on top and oozing down its slopes.

"Sissi, look." Didda stood up, but Sissi kept picking. Didda raised her voice. "Sissi, look at the mountain."

Rubbing her berry-stained hands on the moss, she got up slowly. "I have my pail full. What about the mountain?" Then she turned her head and followed where Didda was pointing.

"Oh no." She whispered.

"Maybe it'll move north." Didda said as they watched and gauged the move of the fog. Looking at each other, they wordlessly agreed that it was coming their way. By the looks of it, they were in for a "soupy one" as Grandpa would say. Putting a pail into each flour sack, they tied the top tight to keep the berries from falling out.

Getting back on their horses, they yelled at the dog to start the cows moving. Old Red moo'ed in protest but reluctantly led the way. The bell on her neck clanged as she started to walk in the hoof-path. Freyja did not want to move, but Blackie knew what to do. He ran yipping from side to side and threatened to nip her legs. The heifer decided to fall in line with Old Red. The third cow, Hilda, followed. Cow-poke-slowly the parade started.

Sissi kept Star close behind Hilda. Didda followed on Rusty and kept twisting and looking back keeping an eye on the fog as it slithered down the crags. She, of course, was expecting to see one or more of the Hidden Folks that materialized in any good, proper fog.

Icy fingers were already playing up and down her spine when she heard an awful sound; baagh, baagh, baagh…

Her blood ran cold, the small hairs on the back of her neck curled up as her heart thumped a mile a minute. Didda whacked Rusty on the rump, moving him out of the rut and up on the bank. Catching up with Sissi, she poked her sister's arm with her horsewhip.

"What's the matter with you?" She asked, startled and a little irritated. "The fog is behind us, I think we can beat it if we can get the cows to move a little faster."

"No, Sissi. Stop, listen. Can't you hear it?" Didda asked frantically.

Sissi stopped her horse and tilted her head just as another bagh, bagh, bagh resounded in the cliffs.

"It doesn't sound scary. I can't quite make it out. Wait. Look at that sheep up there, by that boulder." Sissi pointed. "She's just standing there baa'ing. The other ones around her are eating. Something isn't right." She squinted her eyes, intent on the sheep.

For a moment, Didda stared at the ground by the boulder then recognized the sound. "I think her lamb fell into a hole and is crying down there, that's what makes it sound so weird." Didda turned Rusty and had him take few steps toward the hillside and faced the sheep, but didn't move any further. Then Didda heard the sound again and could tell that indeed it was a lamb in distress. Anxiety replace her fear of the trolls.

"Come on Sissi, we've got to get the lamb out or it will die."

"Let's hurry then! Blackie will get the cows home, and if we get caught in the fog our horses will get us back to the farm."

Quickly, Sissi turned Star out of the rut and joined Didda on the top of the bank. They went across the river and up the gravelly side of the mountain toward the large rock. The ewe warily eyed them as she backed away a few steps, and then stopped. When they came around the boulder, they saw an opening in the ground where the yammering was coming from. As they dismounted, Didda looked with unease at the thick fog that had now drifted with long fingers to the bottom of the valley, slowly obliterating everything in their path.

The girls got down on their stomach and looked into the narrow chasm. The young lamb had left numerous marks where it had tried, in futile attempt, to climb out. From the way it was moving around, it didn't look to have any broken limbs, but was exceedingly nervous.

"It's too deep for us to jump into." Sissi sat back on her haunches and stared sadly at the pathetic little ewe. "We could slide down, but we wouldn't be able to get out of there. The walls are really smooth. There aren't any toeholds."

They sat for a moment contemplating their dilemma. The lamb cred piteously. From the droppings in the hole, Didda surmised the lamb had been there overnight and was very hungry.

"Well, tell you what, I'm taking the bridle off of Rusty. He won't leave."

Didda handed the harness to Sissi. "I'll go down and you hand this to me. I'll catch the lamb and strap it down then lift it up to you. Since I am littler than you, it'll be easier for you to pull me up than for me to pull you."

Dubious, Sissi gnawed at her bottom lip. "Are you sure we should do this Diddamin?"

"We've been in volcanic crevasses before, Sissi. With this fog, no one will be able to get here in time to save the lamb, it will starve to death." Shudder ran down her sister's back, biting her trembling lower lip she nodded. Didda slid down into the hole as Sissi dropped the harness after her, holding the loop end tightly in her hands.

The lamb tried frantically to scramble away as Didda grabbed it, but she desperately held on. Wrapping her arms around it, she held the lamb's feet as it kicked weakly while Didda worked the rope around the white, wooly body. Didda saw the two VV cuts in the left ear and recognized it as Grandpa's mark. Holding tight, she lifted the small lamb to Sissi, who was on her stomach, her hands reaching down.

"Got her." She exulted, working the small ewe from the bridle. Then Didda heard a soft "Oh, she headed straight for mamma." Sissi's head came back into view. She was giggling. "Her stubby tail is a blur she is wagging it so fast. She must have been absolutely starving. She's suckling like there's no tomorrow!"

Didda was happy to hear that, but she was more than ready to get out of this troll-hole.

"Here it comes. I have my feet braced against a rock." Sissi said as the rope slithered down. Didda held on to the loop of the harness and pulled herself up hand-over-hand as her sister grunted loudly, pulled and held on.

They sat on the rim of the fissure for a moment catching their breath. Grinning from ear to ear, they watched the mamma-ewe and her lamb.

They just barely beat the fog. By the time Didda had put the bridle back on Rusty, the grey, soggy mist wrapped around them. The girls remembered the admonition from the family: If you're ever caught in a fog, loosen the hold on the reins and let the horses take over, they'll know the way. They let the horses lead them home where a relieved Grandma greeted them.

That was the last big adventure the sisters had together at Grandpa's farm. A few weeks after the berry picking and lamb rescue, they returned home for the winter. The next year, Didda traveled by herself while her sisters stayed in Reykjavik with their Father and Mother.

CHAPTER 7

Vopnafjörður

They had found her! She could feel the ground tremble as they stomped their giant feet and coming closer and closer. She shot out of the cave where she had been hiding and started running in total panic, faster – faster – faster…but then her legs began to feel like lead, she could barely move. Clenching her fists, she grit her teeth and desperately tried to run, but she was going slower and slower. Her heart felt like it was pounding clear out of her chest. Then the ground shook again and she sensed horrible, bony troll-fingers reaching to grab her…

Startled, Didda jumped upright in bed. What a nightmare. Just then, a jolt shook the bed. She waited a moment, but all was quiet. *Just a small aftershock from the earthquake couple of days ago*, she thought, laying back down.

Suddenly, she remembered. Today was the day, school was over and summer had begun. Anticipation tingled from her head to her curled-up toes. Then, carefully, she untangled her legs from her siblings. Rubbing her eyes, she looked at the sleeping forms. Her older brother, Buddy, was tucked up into a tight ball, his nose scrunched up against the wall. Sissi was on her back, with her hands clasped under her head, dark hair spread out like raven wings. Lilla, sleeping next to Didda, had her knees pulled up to her chin. Her curly blond hair was in damp ringlets at the back of her neck. Didda rubbed the spot in her back where Lilla's heels had been digging into. The four older kids in the same bed, packed end to end like sardines in a tin can, while her baby brother, Frankie slept in a crib in their parent's bedroom.

A sliver of grey daylight showed through a small slit in the dark-brown curtain. Didda Swinging her skinny legs out and eased out from between the cozy-warm top and bottom duvets. The floor was cold, shivering her bare toes hunted for her wooly socks, not bothering to see if she got hers or one of her siblings.

Didda tiptoed quietly into the dusky, grey-lit living room. The quake had had caused a large oil painting of the waterfall, Gullfoss, to hang slightly crooked on the green-painted wall. The copper pendulum on the large Grandfather clock swung with soft, clicking precision, side-to-side, *tick-tock tick-tock*. Nanny Hannah's loud snore came rumbling from the corner where she slept on a cot. The white duvet rose and fell as she breathed slowly and deeply.

Stealthily, Didda slid her feet across the wood planks. A small CRACK sound from a loose board on the floor sounded like a shotgun blast had gone off in the quiet night. Didda froze, her heart rapidly flip-flopped. The snoring stopped. Didda held her breath. Then the quivering, snoring rumble started up again, a notch louder. Nanny Hannah helped Didda's mom with housework and the five children. She was a big woman. Not fat, just big: big hands, big feet, big nose, big eyes and a very big voice. She kept the kids in line with just her voice. None of the kids was ever spanked…but oh the *voice* and *the look*…

Grabbing a black knit shawl from the back of a rocker, she wrapped it tightly around her bony shoulders and crept up to the window. Lifting a corner of the ecru-colored crocheted curtain, she peered out through the dusty pane. The ragged clouds in the pale-blue sky above Mount Esja were streaked and edged with golden-red sunrays above her snow-white top. Grey, eerie shadows floated in and out of her crags and crevasses and gave the mountain a haunted look.

The long, gloomy dark days of winter were beginning to give way to nights that were getting lighter and lighter. Soon they would have twenty-four hours of daylight that would last until mid-August when the cycle of dark winters and bright summer-nights would start again. She looked at the clock; four-thirty. She had a long wait.

Didda glanced down and potted a small blob of quicksilver in the corner of the windowsill; the kids had frustrated themselves for hours with trying to pick up the elusive blobs. Their Father had poured the silver onto the sill after Hanna had accidentally broken a thermometer.

Yawning, Didda pondered the slithery lump then tried to pinch it between her fingers, but it broke into pieces and scattered across the sill in several tiny, silvery balls. Giving up, she curled up on the floor and went back to sleep.

The next morning, she awoke to the delicious aroma of pancakes and cinnamon. Her mother and Nanny Hannah were bustling about preparing breakfast. After last-minute checking of everything and everybody, mother crammed the kids' pockets with kleinurs (twisted cookies). Didda's two travel worn, scratched-up brown suitcases and a bag full of books sat by the back door.

"Time to leave." Mother said, as she picked up little Frankie.

Hannah grabbed the two suitcases while Sissi picked up Didda's bag of books. They all hurried out the door to catch the bus that would take them to downtown Reykjavik. Several people were on the bus and few seat were available, except for the backseat. The adults did not care for the jostling and bouncing of the ancient, dilapidated vehicle and shunned the backseat to the delight of the kids.

"Head for the backseat." Buddy hollered.

Sissi, with bookbag clunking against the seats, Didda, and Lilla followed rambunctiously. After a bumpy, twenty-minute, stop and go ride down to the square, they got off and headed for the dock where the passenger ship, Godafoss II, was anchored.

Didda skipped down the pier to the ship. The harbor was crammed with mixture of fishing vessels of all sizes, both foreign and domestic. Their masts reached to the sky like skinny trees in a forest while a variety of national flags snapped briskly in the stiff breeze. Raucous noise and the steady roar of the ships' crane-engines filled the air as hustling crew loaded and unloaded cargo, shouting directions. Swarms of seabirds swooped and screeched overhead. Their abundant droppings splattered and white-streaked the pier.

Breathing the tangy salty air, and smelling gasoline mixed with hot diesel oil, added to Didda's expectation of adventure. She was on her way to Grandpa's farm - this time all by herself. After much hugging, kissing and admonitions from her mother, she worked her way up the gangplank with other boarding passengers.

Tucking her knit scarf tighter around her neck, she shivered with excitement and a little chill. She yanked up her creeping wool stockings, smoothed down her homemade brown cotton skirt and leaned over the ship's rail searching for her family among the crowd clustered on the dock. A nippy northern gale rippled the dark-blue water of the bay. The seawater sloshed up against the black barnacle-covered pilings, sending freezing-cold sprays over the folks waiting to see the ship off. Didda spotted her family who were huddled together to wish her a good journey. She giggled as see saw her two sisters running for cover, shrieking when they were showered with water. Yanking their sweaters over their heads, they both tried to keep covered and wave at Didda at the same time. As the ship's horn blasted in preparation for departure, Didda watched her little brother cover his ears, as mischievous Buddy stomped both feet in the puddles. She could see that his socks and bottom of his pants were getting soaked as he jumped wildly, laughing and waving. Covering her face as she saw him stumble, she was sure he would go face first into the water, grimy with bird-droppings. Hannah grabbed him before disaster happened. After another blast, the ship began slowly to move away from the pier. Didda waved both hands hopping up and down as the family waved back, the kids jumping and shouting.

"Bless, bless!"

"Have a good trip!"

"See you in a few months!"

The shouting faded away as the ship steamed out of the sheltered harbor. Sailing past the two lighthouses and out of the calm bay, they entered into the rough Atlantic Ocean. Didda watched as her hometown grew smaller and smaller in the distance.

The trip would take them around the south and eastern coast of Iceland, in and out of numerous fjords. It would take several days and nights, if nothing slowed them down and they stayed on schedule. Her mother had arranged for a girl named Sara, who was also traveling on the ship, to look after Didda, until she arrived at her Grandfather's. Didda knew Sara would not treat her like a baby and she would give Didda a lot of freedom. She looked around and, not seeing Sara, started exploring the ship.

As they headed toward their first stop, Vestmannaeyjar (Vestmann-aye yah), the green-blue sea became choppy and the ship began a set of roller coaster-moves in the waves. The ocean fanned out like wings on either side of the bow, sending streams of foamy, salty water into the air. Didda loved to stand at the front rail and pretend she was a figurehead like on the ships of old, stretching her neck and pointing her nose into the air, feeling the misty spray soak her face. She licked her lips, savoring the taste of brine.

As the ship sailed closer to their destination Didda could see white, frothy sprays shoot high up into the air as the ocean crashed fiercely against the massive, sheer cliffs, then is swirled back into eddies of receding waves only to send another booming surge against the rocks.

Thousands of seagulls, krias, gannets, puffins, and other seabirds soared in the cloud-covered sky. Some of the birds seemingly hung in the air by an invisible string; others would dive straight down like a fallen star, totally disappear into the tumultuous waves, and then come flying up with a wriggling trophy in their beak. How can they do that? Didda was quite intrigued. Why don't they drown? Grandpa is smart and knows so much, I'll have to ask him.

CHAPTER 8

Vestmannaeyar & The Trölls at Vik

The mournful-sounding blast from the horn of the Godafoss II announced their entry into the fjord. The boom echoing and bouncing off the towering cliffs that sheltered the harbor and sending gazillions of birds into the air screeching manically in fluttering frenzies. Starchy puffins, with their huge red-and-yellow gaudy colored beaks sat on the edges of the cliffs, perched on numerous ledges, and the steep rock walls. There were puffins fishing in the ocean and puffins clumsily flying low over the ship, baby-eels in their beak. Didda stared, there were puffins everywhere.

She gazed at the knot of people gathered on the pier, suitcases grasped in their hands and boxes at their feet. As the ship slowly navigated the harbor, a few stragglers, mostly kids, were running down the unpaved, lava-cinder covered street. Fine black dust flew up and swirled in the not-yet-bright sunlight. Didda watched as some of the kids stopped and carefully grabbed a few wayward pufflings on the wharf and dropped the baby birds back into the ocean to be reunited with their mammas, who were anxiously swimming in circles.

Excitement escalated and folks began to shout and wave as the ship eased up to the dock. Passengers gathered at the port side as the gangplank was lowered for those that were leaving and those that were coming aboard. All the while, there was grunting and the hustle of the crew as they loaded and unloaded freight. It was a lively, noisy scene; droning of the engine of ship's crane, directions shouted as cargo was moved, and the clamor as folks shouted to one another.

The stop was brief. With much waving and hollering of "Bless, bless" they again headed out to the open sea and toward the southeast tip of Iceland. The harbor of Höfn (Ho-fn) and their next stop.

With a book in hand, Didda found her favorite place, the bow of the ship, where she'd rather be although the air was chilly. Most of the passengers preferred the comfort of being inside drinking coffee and Brennivin [Fire Wine], also called Black Death because of its potency. She had heard the story of an old drink-hardened sailor from another country who had taken a swig and had to run six kilometers to getting his breath back.

Drowsily, she dropped the book to her lap to gaze idly at the coast. She dreamily pondered the mountains and the glaciers on the mainland as the ship sailed on by. She watched with quickened interest as Eyjafjallajökull and Mýrdalsjökull came into view. Both glaciers had volcanoes hiding beneath their ice caps. It was just a matter of time until they would blow their tops. Hopefully, not as wickedly as old Hekla, which lurked menacingly a few miles inland, her perpetual cloud obscuring her top. In the old Sagas, she was called the Gateway to Hell. Didda shuddered.

Suddenly, she felt the hairs on the back of her neck standing straight up and her skin crawled. Bolting upright, she stared at the sea-stacks out in the ocean between the ship and land. Two of those stacks were from Gryla's family - the worse tröll of all Icelandic trolls. The trölls had tried to snatch a three-mast ship that was sailing in these waters. Everyone knew the story of how the trölls had tried to drag the ship ashore to Vik. The valiant crew fought back courageously and slowed the troll's progress. They slowed them enough that the sun came up and turned the trölls into stone. All that was left of the two trölls were those stone-stacks Didda saw.

Puffing out a deep sigh Didda relaxed as the Godafoss steamed full speed ahead toward Hofn and the trölls were swallowed in a shroud of grey, foggy mist. She shivered in relief as they disappeared from her sight.

The coast of the mainland was hazy but she could still see the majestic, panoramic view of the largest glacier in Iceland, Vatnajokull. It rose dramatically into the air, the top barely visible in wispy shreds of fog. As she watched, an ice boulder the size of a house broke from the glacier and came tumbling down the glacial river. Hurtling into the Atlantic the boulder broke into smaller chunks. Mesmerized, she watched the back and forth fight as the ocean waves pushed the ice back into the mouth of the river, only to have the river spew the ice back out to the ocean. The river won - Didda saw the chunks of ice being tossed about in the sea, and then thrown up against the rocky headlands as the relentless waves showered the black lava rocks.

Hugging herself and drawing her knees to her chest, she stared in fascination as Humpback whales' spouts exploded like miniature Geysers, white-dotted the ocean. Seals lolled about on small volcanic skerries (tiny rock islands) and dolphins shot up in graceful arch, their wet backs glistening, as a flock of screeching gulls hovered over them. A gaggle of honking geese added to the melee.

The ship slowed as it approached the harbor and Didda regarded at the familiar town. The village of Hofn was small. Numerous fish-racks were scattered at the edge of the pier with cod hanging out to dry. The fishy smell saturated the air. Arctic terns and seagulls clustered and circled above the racks, diving down and pecking at the fish.

Running children were so heavily bundled up in bulky sweaters that Didda could not tell boys from girls. They scrambled on the brownish-colored rocks, slipping on the slick algae, yelling and chasing the screeching birds that would fly up in the air, and then come back down fluttering their wings and hopping on the racks.

Small rowboats and larger fishing vessels anchored in a seemingly hazardous manner. The small boats smacked the sea as they bounced up and down in the incoming waves. A small group of men from the village had gathered to watch the activity on the dock. Some were mending their nets draped among the numerous strong-smelling fish barrels. Puffing on their pipes, they occasionally glanced at the horizon and murmured amongst themselves. Their pipes, clamped between their teeth, bobbed up and down as they spoke. Tobacco smoke floated in the air, the whiff blended with the salty smell of the ocean and the rank odor of haddock, herring and other fish.

Didda noticed one passenger came aboard, a woman, but no one disembarked. It did not take long for the energetic and experienced crew to unload cargo. Soon they left Hofn and headed back out.

So far, the sea had been moderately calm, most of the time. As the Godafoss II made its way past the peninsula and headed north, past the island of Papey and toward Djupivogur, their next stop, the wind became northeasterly. Swiftly rolling, dark-grey ominous looking clouds appeared on the horizon.

CHAPTER 9

The East Fjords

Suddenly the northeast wind came barreling across the ocean and the Godafoss II began to pitch and roll as the heaving waves became more boisterous. Some of the passengers started to get seasick and throw up over the side of the ship before dashing to their rooms below deck. To Didda's relief, the violent pitch-and-roll did not last long. Once the ship entered the sheltered fjord, the sea calmed and the plunging lessened.

Djupivogur was typical of the eastern fjords, Didda mused as she took in the picturesque fishing village surrounded by tall, ruggedly eerie mountains of hardened lava that plunged straight into the deep fjord. Numerous brightly painted fishing boats were anchored everywhere - by the dock, near the dock, away from the dock. Red and black painted boats, white and black, green and black, some were peeling and badly in need of paint. Others were freshly painted.

The air was filled with hovering screeching seagulls and the, even more raucous and aggressive, arctic bird, kria. As always, they were greedily fighting over any morsels that passengers tossed overboard.

The usual loading and unloading took place while new passengers came aboard. Didda became interested in watching one of them. He looked about twenty years old and had a cheerful round ruddy face. A navy-blue stocking cap was pulled over long, reddish-blonde, hair that curled over the collar of his black jacket. His grey sack was tied up with dirty white rope and slung over his left shoulder. In his right hand, he carried a brown, beat-up, square-shaped case secured with rope, badly frayed from being tied and re-tied.

She wondered if it was an accordion case. Her Uncle Bibbi had an accordion case very similar to that. Maybe they would have a rollicking Polka-dance. It would be hilarious to watch people try to dance while the ship tossed them around like puppets on a string. Didda laughed to herself as she imagined the riotous scene.

Easing away from the pier, the Godafoss II headed out of the fjord toward the open east Atlantic. Turning north and stopping at smaller villages along the way they soon arrived at Reydarfjordur. They passed men and boys in small fishing boats and one in a rowboat, their fishing lines trailed alongside. The occupants waved in cheerful greeting. Some of the passengers waved back.

After the Godafoss II had docked, a few passengers got off. One older man took his time ambling down; no one was there to greet him and a woman who, firmly, walked down the gangplank. Her black hair pulled into a tight bun at the back of her head; an off-white straw hat perched precariously on top of her crown. Black ribbon on the hat flopped up and down as she walked with deliberate steps. She carried a brown leather valise in her left hand as she steadied herself at the handrail with her right and stepped onto the pier. An enthusiastic, young-looking group quickly surrounded her. She looks so prim. I bet she is a school-teacher. Didda watched the group walk toward row of houses.

At the usual blast of the ship's horn, Didda turned and found a chair to sit on as they skirted around the eastern-most part of Iceland, a huge outcrop named Gerpir. Great hulking masses of volcanic cliffs reared up. Heaving waves broke furiously on their sides. Powerful waters swirled up crags then hurled back down into the sea. Wide-eyed, Didda gaped at the fantastic lava formations of turrets and spirals, poking troll-like fingers into the low-lying clouds. Chilling flutter crawled up her spine as she gazed at the grim black rock and thought of the massive eruption that had taken place so long ago.

A strong gale again was whipping up as they headed toward Seydisfjordur, after which they had two small fjords to stop at. Didda was getting anxious. They had been in and out of numerous fjords for four days and three nights and should be on time if nothing slowed the ship. She observed the crew working with unusual haste and wondered if the weather report was bad. She felt anxiety creep into her stomach and hoped there would be no delay.

Sara, her companion, suggested they take a walk along the pier.

Didda agreed; glad to exercise her land-legs for a while. Avoiding dogs fighting with the ever-present greedy noisy gulls, they made their way to an old, orange-painted corrugated lean-to. A red-enamel chipped coffeepot, with a hearty steam billowing from the spout, sat on a rough semblance of a counter made from pieces of driftwood. Several tin mugs and a bowl of sugar-cubes were at one end. A smiling couple greeted them and introduced themselves as Ketill and wife Sturla, owners of the Kaffihus (coffeehouse). The couple offered them air-dried fish to munch on, hot coffee for Sara and a mug of hot milk with sugar cubes for Didda.

Wrapping her fingers around the cup she carefully blew and sipped on her hot milk, wishing it was coffee. She did not ask for any, knowing that some folks thought she was too young. Looking out the grimy window, she watched as four men and a young boy were working on a small fishing boat. It looked to her that they were preparing to sail.

"Hey Ingi, I hear the weather report isn't so good." Their host had stepped out the door and bellowed as he buttoned up his heavy, yellow slicker. "Not planning to go fishing, are you?"

"Yah, but it won't be a winter storm this time of the year, snuff and coffee on me when we get back, Ketill." Ingi grinned and touched his black cap smartly as he entered his pilothouse.

Ketill grimaced, scratching his scraggly beard. He squinted hard and stared at the grey-black clouds rolling even more aggressively across the horizon.

"I have a bad feeling." He muttered.

Sturla, standing behind her husband, pushed wind-blown strands of auburn hair from her face as her left hand nervously twisted a corner of her long, black apron.

"I can't believe my sister would let her youngest go on that boat today. Ragnar is only ten."

Her brown eyes were shiny with unshed tears. Didda felt sorry for her, but she knew that children in her country started working at a very young age, most were self-reliant and independent. Fishing put food on the table and the ocean was good to Icelanders but it could also be a cold-hearted, merciless enemy.

Thanking the couple for the refreshment, Didda and Sara followed the other passengers who had started back to the ship. Didda's eyes followed the little fishing boat that seemed swallowed up at times in the roiling ocean.

The Godafoss II was at the mouth of the fjord when Sara pointed to Ingi's boat. They watched as the waves pitched the boat high on top of a crest, pausing for a moment then taking a slow, steep descent into a swell and disappearing, only to rise so high that they could see the red-painted bottom of the boat and enormous hills of water streaming off the deck. Again, the boat disappeared. Sara tightened her grip on Didda's shoulder. Didda had never experience such a sinking, horrible tension. She held her breath. Then slowly, like rising out of a watery grave, Ingi's boat appeared. Didda blew out a deep breath of relief and released the white-knuckled grip she had on the rail. The ship turned north and they did not see the boat again.

CHAPTER 10

The Monster Worm

The low, menacing clouds on the northeast horizon blended with the surface of the leaden, heaving sea. The Godafoss II began to seriously pitch and roll, sending heavy mist of spray over the deck. Sara and Didda ran for shelter by one of the lifeboats.

"Let's go inside." Sara wiped her face with her scarf. Didda shook her head, her eyes riveted on the huge waves.

"I'll go and get us something hot to drink." Sara smiled as she left. Didda watched her leave and thought how glad she was that her mother had picked this woman to be her companion. She had looked out for her but at the same time respected Didda's independence. Her neat, light-brown hair and slightly squinty, faded-blue eyes made her look very plain, but when she smiled with that extra-wide mouth of hers, she had the sunniest expression. Didda liked her and knew she would miss her as she continued on to Akureyri, where she had a governess job waiting.

Didda grabbed a rope as a sudden pitch tilted the ship and she began toppling sideways. Her heart flopped crazily. With spine-tingling sensation, her mind went to her father. Last winter he had been a crew-member on a fishing trawler on its way to Liverpool, England. They had just passed the Isla of Man when a winter storm caught them. The ship sank with seven men on board. Didda remembered how, after that, she had nightmares of perils and shipwrecks that replacing her favorite dreams. The favorite dreams of traveling far away, across the wide ocean and on a safari in Africa where she would sit fanning herself with a huge palm-leaf when someone approaches and says, "Doctor Jonasdottir, I presume…"

"Hot milk" Sara's voice startled Didda out of her daydreaming. She let go of the rope she had been holding on to and reached for the cup, just as a fierce Nor'easter struck. A stinging, raw, numbing drizzle, mixture of sleet and rain right out of the arctic stung their cheeks. It forced them to take one last look then, shivering, scuttle inside, shaking their drenched sweaters.

The captain and the crew were now battling the elements in earnest. Didda could barely hear the shouting of the crew over the screeching cables and howling gale.

Didda spilled her milk as she ran. She settled in the dining area, watching the storm as it blasted outside the window. A steward re-filled her cup of milk and gave her pancakes filled with whipped cream and jelly. Suddenly, the plunging and the pitching of the ship threw a metal coffeepot clanking to the floor, sending splatters of coffee on the walls, ceiling and floor. Glasses slid across tables while people were frantically trying to grab them. Flying forks, knives and spoons were clattering every which way. The whipping cream in her pancake slath-ered a stool as she squeezed it into a gooey mess between her fingers.

Sara grabbed her as they were all thrown around like ragdolls. Men were uttering swear words under their breath, others bellowing and grumbling.

"It's the first week of June and we're in the middle of a winter-snowstorm; only in Iceland do you go through four seasons in one day."

The shrieking of the wild wind and the yelling of the crew was getting unnerving when Svenni, the passenger from Seydisfjordur, reached for his case and opened it up. Didda clapped her hands when she saw Svenni lift out an accordion. In no time, his fingers were fly-ing over the keys and pounding out rollicking polka. There was not enough room for everyone to get up and dance, but Didda though they probably would have ended up flopping on the floor anyway. They stomped their feet and thumped their hands in beat with the music as they crashed into one another with every roll of the ship. It was a real neck-snapping time. They started belting out favorite folk songs - if not forgetting the ferocious weather, at least ignoring it for a time. The bedlam went on for hours and they all started getting hoarse from the singing.

All of a sudden, in mid-song, Svenni stopped, and cocked his head. "Listen..."

It was almost eerily quiet. Didda heard the creaking of the ship, still rolling and pitching, but not quite as violently. The booming of the foghorn blasted out. FOGHORN… That had to mean the wind had changed directions, warmer air brought fog!

The men scrambled out the door, the women clambered right behind, holding unto whatever they could as the Godafoss plunged through another billowing wave. They had sailed past Husey, Borgar fjordur and were slowly skirting Heradsfloi. Big and small ice floes tumbled and swayed in the churning ocean. The top of Mount Smjorfjoll was hidden in fog but Didda knew that on the other side was the fjord and village of Vopnafjordur.

Didda was very excited until she saw the ice ahead of them. She heard one crew member say that fishing boats were stranded in ice in the fjord. What if one of them was Grandpa's boat?

She began to pester Sara, "Do you think we'll get in there? Do you think there's to much ice?"

Didda was close to tears. She moved away from Sara and the other passengers who were milling around, some glaring at her with obvious frustration. Adults in Iceland had little patience for crying children.

Finding a spot where she could be by herself, Didda stared at the constantly heaving waters. She thought perhaps the Monster Worm, Lagarfljotsormurinn, was lost and thrashing about, trying to find his way back home. Everyone knew he lived in Lake Lagarfljót. The Godafoss II was not far from where the Lagarfljót River emptied into the bay. Fearful, Didda peered into the waves, wanting to, and not wanting to spot this awful monster. It was said to bode ill tidings if a person saw the Monster Worm when it reared its back out of the water. She knew all about it because her Uncle Bibbi had told her the legend of this monster.

Many centuries ago, when Iceland was new, a mother gave her little girl a gold ring. The girl asked her mom how she could make the gold grow. The mother told her to put a small worm on the ring and place it inside a box to make the gold grow. The girl did as her mother told her. Later, when the little girl went to check how much the gold had grown, she found that along with the gold growing, the worm had also grown. It was now a huge scary dragon. Terrified, the girl flung the box, ring and worm into Lake Lagarfljot where it continued to grow and eventually became the huge monster-dragon that terror-ized folks living on the east coast of Iceland. They called it the Monster Worm - and that lake was not far from Grandpa's farm.

"EEEK" Didda screamed as she jumped threw her hands up in the air. She had been so absorbed in her imagination that she had not been aware of Sara, who walked up and touched her shoulder. "You scared the daylights out of me!"

"You're gripping the rails so hard your knuckles are white." She looked concerned. "What's the matter? Your Mother said you had traveled the fjords since you were six. You must be used to all kinds of weather and we are past the worst. What is it?" She asked softly.

Didda started to tell her about the worm, but then realized Sara had answers for everything, even the unexplainable. In previous con-versation with her, Didda knew Sara did not believe in trolls, elves or Hidden People.

"The weather has been so awful, I just wondered if the little boat in Seydisfjordur made it home safely." Didda's lips trembled, but she held back tears. She was also thinking of her Grandpa and the boats stranded in the ice.

"Yes dear, all we can do is to hope and pray that they are all right." Sara patted Didda's shoulder. "Goodness, look at that soupy fog roll in," She exclaimed.

The Godafoss had slowed to a stop. Didda could now see Butter Mountain peaks white-dusted with snow. Fingers of fog were swirling thickly, reaching into clefts and crevasses of the lunar-like landscape. She could barely make out a few sheep grazing on the incredibly dif-ficult, steep mountainside.

The thickening fog shrouded the ship. Crewmembers and passen-gers looked like ghostly spooks as they moved about. The heavy mist gave Didda a feeling of being wrapped in wet, grey gauze. Staring into the thick fog, she could see eerie faces - hollow black holes for eyes, long curvy noses, and creepy bony fingers curled to grab.

Her imagination was in high gear as she backed into Sara, who promptly claimed that she was wet and would get her death from cold. Didda looked at her, disgusted. This woman has absolutely no imagination. Ducking into their room, Didda changed into a warm sweater, dry skirt, and black wooly socks. She threw her wet clothes over the heavy cord Sara had strung across the small cabin. Didda watched for a moment as clothes swung and swayed with every roll of the sea, then went back out to the upper deck. Breezy gusts had lifted the fog quite a bit. It was still very cold. Ice floes the size of grown sheep were pumping up against the sides of the ship causing unnerving sound - a creaking, grinding, scraping noise.

Uneasy, Didda watched as the tide and movements of the ocean caused the ice to sway, bounce and head away from land. Hearing the engines start up again and feeling the vibration, Didda hugged herself in anticipation. Only a few more hours and she would see her family again.

CHAPTER 11

The Fjord is Alive with Seals and Ice

The Godafoss II snaked its way slowly along the coast to avoid icepacks. As it rounded Hellisheid Cliff and entered the fjord of Vopnafjordur, exclamations of unbelief rumbled up and down at the rails of the ship as passengers gathered in awe. The fjord was alive with tumbling, rolling, bobbing ice chunks and floes.

"Oh look, the seals are going for a ride on the ice, isn't that cute." A woman cooed.

"I wonder if there are any polar bears. Wouldn't that be something," one man muttered.

The ship, or perhaps the noise of the people, must have bothered the seals. They began to scoot off the ice and flop into the sea; their large, shiny eyes looked at the humans curiously, as they swam away. The combination of ebb tide and flowing of the ocean was moving the ice pack to the mouth of the fjord. Didda followed one large mass with her eyes. She wondered if it would reach the Fareyar Islands. It might even get to Norway, but by then it might be reduced to an itsy-bitsy piece. She wondered how long it would take a chunk like that to melt, whether or not the seals would get back on for a ride and whether the ice would disappear from under them when it melted.

Didda was mulling this over when she noticed a wrecked fishing vessel lying on its side, half-submerged in the ocean. Her stomach lurched as she saw the exposed, black-painted stern, waves washing over it in great sloshing gushes. Then she noticed the Norwegian flag painted on the side. She felt guilty at the feeling of relief that warmed her body. This wasn't Grandpa's boat.

Didda was ecstatic when they finally arrived at the dock. Aunt Thora gave her a tight bear hug as she got off the ship, then pushed her back, looked, and grabbed her again rocking side to side. Didda always felt special when she was with her aunt and uncle, they did not have any children and treated her as if she was a daughter.

Aunt Thora was wearing her blue and white-striped nurses' dress. She had taken off her white apron and stiff cap. Her short black hair with its wide patch of white made her noticeable from a distance. Close up, her brown right eye and blue left eye, just like Grand-Amma's, were both warm and welcoming. Uncle Olaf stood nearby, looking typically bedraggled with his large brown sweater drooping unevenly below his waist.

Sara had been standing close and Didda remembered now to introduce her. Together, the small group ambled toward a small-corrugated metal building where coffee was being served. When Olaf heard Sara was on her way to Akureyri to be a governess, he wanted to know the name of the family. Hearing it, he told her he knew the family quite well. Akureyri had been his hometown growing up. After visiting for a while, they all walked back to the ship to see Sara off. She glanced over to the wreck of the Norwegian boat, and then gazed at Thora with a questioning look. Didda's aunt nodded.

"We have three of them at the infirmary. The rest we weren't able to save."

Thora looked away, but Didda saw the single tear that that trickled down her left cheek. Sara reached over and gave Thora a sympathetic hug as the whistle for departure split through the air.

Grabbing Didda tightly she laughed "Bless, bless elska min." She gave a droll wink as she chuckled, "And don't daydream too much."

After embracing Thor and the Olaf, Sara walked swiftly up the gangplank. As she stepped on the deck, she turned, waved, and blew them a kiss. Didda knew she was going to miss her friend.

Olaf reached down and picked up Didda's two suitcases. Thora stepped away to inquire about medical supplies she was expecting. The crewmember told her the box was already unloaded and waiting at the warehouse nearby. They walked past a couple of empty, corrugated sheds that were so weather-beaten that it was impossible to tell the original paint color. The warehouse was in better shape. The wood front was freshly painted white. A window and the extra-wide door were red-trimmed, matching the red corrugated roof. Several people where milling around inside as they entered the door. Many started to ask about the survivors.

"Thora, over here, I have your supplies."

The roar came from a bear of a man who towered over everyone. His huge red beard drooped down his chin and his fiery red hair stuck out from his head as he had stuck a finger into an electric socket.

"How are the Norwegians doing? It's too bad we couldn't get to all of them, but," His voice was rough as it boomed from his massive chest. Didda cringed and snuck behind Olaf.

"Scared the little one." He said. "Sorry. Anyway, here is your box, Thora. Not very heavy."

"Thank you, Halldor." Thora said as she turned and looked at the folks who had been asking about her patients.

"All but one are doing well, but I'm sure they'll recover soon and be able to rejoin their families." Thora smiled as she and Olaf walked out the door with fuming Didda behind them. Little one, hmmp! She was big enough to travel by herself for five days and four nights. Well, almost by herself. She was no little one!

Thora glanced at Didda's kicking feet raising the dust. "I need to have coffee roasted and ground when we get home. I'm almost out."

She spoken to Olaf but Didda knew she meant that the comment was meant for her. Aunt Thora knew grinding coffee beans was her absolute favorite job. They walked past the church where old Snorri rang the bell every Sunday morning. It did not matter if it was winter, if there was snow or sleet or a perfect summer day, he was there without fail. Every Sunday that Didda was with Thora and Olaf, they attended that little Lutheran church.

As they walked towards the infirmary, Didda glanced to her left. The wide inlet of the fjord was still heaving and splashing against the rugged coast. Huge columns of powerful sprays shot up into the air, making the seabirds screech like crazy, especially the gulls. Through the mist, Didda could see Butter Mountain reach grandly to the sky. There was less snow on her peaks than the other side where they had sailed past a few hours before.

The steep, basalt rock-wall rose high on their right side as they walked toward the house. Several ptarmigans sat on ledges in the crevasses, their white winter feathers beginning to turn a summer-speckled brown. Walking by them did not disturb them at all.

Kristjan, the shoemaker, had a small house and shoe-making

shack on top of that cliff. Finna, his eleven-year-old daughter ran out hollering and waving at Didda, as her high-pitched voice echoed in the crags.

Didda waved back and then had to grab her aunt's skirt to keep from falling as she stumbled. Her eyes darted everywhere except on the road as she was thinking how she and Finna, instead of using the road, would climb up and down the sheer lava cliff by finding a gritty lava ledge in which to stick their toes or grip with their fingers. At times, the brittle shale would break off with heart-stopping suddenness that sent their adrenalin racing. For a moment, it would scare them half to death, but it was never enough to stop them from using this precarious mode of visiting one another, and perchance picking few bird eggs.

She was now getting quite anxious, as they got closer to the house-hospital. She wanted everything to be the same as it was last year.

CHAPTER 12

Viking Kids Don't Cry

The two corrugated sheds where Didda had tried to get her sister, Lilla, to jump from were askew from the earthquake last year, but still standing. As she ran ahead of Aunt Thora and Olaf and towards the house, Didda thought, *I could still jump from one to the other*. A low moaning-groan greeted her. She skidded to a stop, her heart thumping wildly. Then the moaning faded to a grunt, and she heard a voice.

"I'm sorry, just one more bandage and I'll be through." A woman said gently.

A man's gruff voice said something. Didda did not understand the words but she understood the groaning. She assumed the voice must belong to one of the patients. He must be hurting bad! Her heart stopped pounding as she realized what the moaning was. She turned as Thora dropped the box on the table and went into the sickroom.

Although she did not speak Norwegian, she had been around sailor-fishermen enough to recognize the language. She could hear her Aunt speaking, it sounded as if she had asked a question. The man's voice answered in a loud voice that, Didda thought, sounded belligerent. Her aunt came out of the room with a big grin.

"Hans wants to get up and walk around!" She gleefully told Olaf. "He is getting so much better."

"He sure groaned a lot for someone who is getting better. He scared the wits out of me!" Didda said looking around the room, still feeling a little freaked out.

A tall, rawboned, and very capable-looking woman came into the kitchen. Her abundant orange-red hair stuck out in all directions. It reminded Didda of Halldor's hair, the big man down at the warehouse.

"Hallo there and you must be the visitor from Reykjavik." Cocking her head, she measured Didda up from her shoes to the top of her head with piercing green eyes.

"You are one spunky girl, aren't you? I am Sigga." Sticking out her calloused, very large right hand. Her enormous hands engulf Didda's smaller ones. They shook hands like two adults. She did not call her a little one, not a little girl, but spunky. Didda liked the sound of it; it was not wimpy.

"I'm pleased to meet you. My name is Ieda." Didda said politely, just as she had been taught. "Thora is my aunt and Olaf is my uncle." She added primly.

"Ieda. That is an unusual name. I like it." Sigga smiled broadly, as she seated herself in the rocking chair.

"I don't like my name at all." Didda grumbled, drawing her dark eyebrows in a tight knot. "People are always saying it wrong. They say Yta, or Ita, even Ida. The kids at school make fun of it and rhyme it with bad words." Didda frowned, gnawing the inside of her mouth. "Grandpa said I was supposed to be named after Aunt Thora. He says my name is outlandish. He calls me Didda or Diddamin. No one ever heard of my real name, whatever that is." Didda stared at the floor.

Her eyes felt hot. *I'm not going to be a cry-baby, Grandpa always said that Viking children never cried; they howled, screamed or bellowed but did not cry!* Didda clenched her jaw and rubbed the floor with her toe.

"Your name must be hidden." Sigga mused, rubbing her left thumb over her lower lip. Thora's chair scraped loudly on the floor as she shoved away from the table, clearing her throat.

"What?" Startled, Didda lifted her head and looked into Sigga's face. She had her head tilted, her left eye scrunched shut, looking first at Thora then at Didda.

Leaning close, her wild hair shook like birds shaking bush-leaves as she lowered her voice. In a secretive whisper-like voice, she murmured. "No one in Iceland has heard of your name, right?"

Didda nodded. "That's right."

"No one seems to spell it correctly, right?" Her nose was just two inches from Didda's nose. Puzzled, she nodded again and looked at her aunt, who cleared her throat again, this time quite loudly.

"So, you're not named after anyone in the family?"

Pursing her lips, Didda shook her head vigorously.

Sigga stared Auntie straight in the eye as she leaned back, wiggled, and made herself more comfortable in the rocker. She softly brushed a strand of hair from Didda's face as she lifted her onto her lap. Rocking gently for a moment she got a far-away look on her face then began to speak.

"Once upon a time, eons ago, in the kingdom of the misty *Thule the Hidden* realm, the first Monarch ever had a gorgeous newborn. Her rainbow-hued hair was in tight ringlets that sat on her head like a coronet. She had multi-colored freckles all over her opaque body. She was an extremely unique looking baby." Sigga stopped, coughed, and then continued.

"The King and Queen decided that they must choose an exceptional name for their child. The elf queen, Hilda of Alborg, had warned them that a certain tröll was planning a changeling attack. The trölls plotted to sneak into the palace and switch the King's baby with a tröll baby. When the tröll baby grew up and became Queen, the trölls could take over the land. To thwart the attack, The Elf Queen Hilda suggested that a secret name be given to the child. The King knew a changeling could not take the place of a real child unless the child's name was used in a chant. The King heeded the Elf Queen's advice and gave the baby a name no one knew except the baby's Guardian Angel. The name was kept secret until the end of days. To everyone around her, the child was known by the name of Snotra. This was an elf name that would be a charm and protect the child all through her life."

She stopped for a moment, took a deep breath and with a piercing look at Didda said, "Perhaps your mother heard of this and gave you an unusual name, for charm and good luck."

"Sigga!" Thora started. The chair legs tottered and clattered as she abruptly stood up. She stopped when Sigga glared at her.

"You let me finish, Thora." Then turned back to Didda. "And the kids at school? What do they know? Pouf to their opinions name-calling, give it to the trolls!" She waved her hand and snapped her fingers.

Didda thought, *Wow, I love this woman! When I get back to school and they start the teasing, I'll just say 'I gave your opinions to the trolls'. I bet that will scare them witless! In just a few moments, a woman I just met took care of my name dilemma just like that.* Didda tried to snap her fingers like Sigga did...*hmmm I'll have to learn to do that!*

Didda scooted off Sigga's lap and ran for the door. She had to share this with Finna. Then she turned and gave Sigga a fierce hug until she grunted, then laughed.

"Diddamin, don't take this story seriously." Aunt Thora called after her, looking very concerned.

"Oh but it's very good, and the kids won't know if it's true or not. We have so many stories like this, but this one is simply the best." Didda giggled as she sped out the door.

The grin stayed plastered on her face as she clambered all the way up the cliff. Wadding the skirt around her knees Didda, raced toward Finna's house. She liked Finna. She had lots of shiny, auburn hair and blue-green eyes that sparkled with merriment. They were the same age, but Finna was three inches taller and weighed more than Didda. She lived with her father, just the two of them. Finna's mother had died when she was only five and Finna did not remember her at all. Her father was a good shoemaker but a stern, taciturn man who had not married again.

Finna listened to Didda with much glee, dancing around the room and clapping her hands, "I kept telling you that you a special name! Your mother was very smart" Then she stopped, a pensive look on her face. "I miss having a mother."

Didda hugged her friend. "You have dad, and you have me." She giggled, "And if you really need her, you can borrow Aunt Thora sometimes."

"Oh, thank you!" Finna said theatrically, giving Didda an exaggerated bow. Then she cocked her head, "Maybe you will help me now. I want to go to the country-dance that's coming up, but I have outgrown my dresses. I have fabric, but I can't cut it out on myself. Dad can't do it." She paused, looked at Didda and asked, "Would you cut it for me?"

Didda was clever with the sewing needle and had made quite a few sock-doll clothes. She was not sure she could do this, but looking into the wistful face of her friend, she knew she had to try.

"Of course I will help you."

A short time later, she was draping the fabric on Finna's body and pinning in place. After everything was just right, Didda cut the fabric. Scraps fell to the floor as she re-fitted and re-pinned the fabric. She snipped away until she was satisfied. Not having a sewing machine,

Didda took prepared fabric home and sewed the dress by hand. She was very proud of her efforts and Finna was excited to have a new dress. It turned out quite pretty and Finna was very happy.

The girls attended the dance together, where they took turns dancing with young men, old men, women and other girls. The old wood floor buckled and popped under their energetic, polka-stomping feet. They danced almost through the whole night. No one wanted to waste the day-bright nights of the short summer.

Grandpa's Farm

Squinting and shading her eyes, Didda searched the white-capped ocean waves for her grandfather's small, black-and-white painted fishing boat. Turning her head, she tried to hear the chug-chug over the screeching of sea gulls and the slapping of the ocean swells as they hit the rocks. She watched as patches of grey fog twirled over the choppy waves in the formidable northern fjord. Leaning forward, she scrunched her eyes almost shut but saw no sign of his boat.

Standing on the edge of the distorted, odd-shaped lava cliff, she felt the ground tremble and heard the powerful ocean crashing and rumbling up the gorge. Swooshing, sucking sounds came from deep within a cave the ocean waves had carved out eons past. Scrambling down a gravelly crevasse, Didda dug in her heels and gripped sharp, lava ledges with her fingers. Scattered clumps of heather bravely tried to find roots in small beds of smooth volcanic ash, the small pink and white flowers contrasting oddly with the blue-grey surrealistic surrounding.

The racket of rolling stones alarmed some nesting puffins, warily they pointed toward Didda with their red, yellow and black-striped, huge beaks. Shaking their short wings and portly bodies, they waddled off on their fiery-red feet.

Didda touched a moss-lined sea gull's nest, which promptly came alive with necks stretching and twitching, hungry mouths wide open. She jerked her hand back as the angry mama-bird streaked down like a meteorite, yellow beak wide open and screaming fiercely.

Carefully avoiding white streaks of yucky bird-droppings and inching her way to the bottom of the cliff, she started running on the narrow strip of gray-black volcanic sand. Her sheepskin shoes made squishy, slushy sounds as small waves wet her feet. A gross smell rose when she kicked against slimy patches of algae and hopped around carcasses of birds, crabs, brittle fish bones and blue seashells.

Stopping for a moment, she leaned against a half-buried relic of a rowboat. Pulling at the coarse, brown fishnet that hung over the rotted bulwark, she disturbed five napping Harbor seals. They looked at her, then moaned, groaned and grumbled before they closed their brown, marble-shiny eyes.

Tugging a yellow seaman's rain hat out of her pocket, Didda fit it tightly over her hair to try to avoid bird droppings as a gazillion seagulls swept overhead. The wispy shreds of fog across the water were slowly dissipating as the sun broke through the clouds. A brilliant gold, red and blue colored rainbow curved over a tall misty waterfall. Rivers and brooks cascaded down the jagged, immense snow-capped mountain sheltering the fjord.

Didda climbed to her favorite place, the top of a barnacle-crusted lava rock accessible on one side in the outgoing tide. Waves caused spray to slosh on Didda's face and sting her cheeks and when she licked her lips, she tasted the brine.

A fog-shrouded steam-ship made its way across the mouth of the fjord. The warning blast of the ships' foghorn boomed mournfully between the basalt, towering cliffs. Powerful spouts from Humpback whales dotted the sea. They slapped their long flippers, roiled the water and made it difficult for Didda to spot grandpa's small boat.

Grey seals shot up out of the ocean, grabbing squirming fish from the beaks of diving gulls. The seals' bodies glistened and shone like well-polished whale bone as they leaped up and then dove back into the waves. Didda watched for a while, mesmerized, then scanned the fjord again, her stomach churned. She knew the deadly perils of the sea. She had heard that Ingi and his crew had drowned in Seydisfjord; shortly after the Godafoss had turned north. She shuddered at the thought of how close she and Sara had been to seeing that happen.

Dragging her feet, she turned back. A virtual blizzard of puffins and seagulls floated above her head. Slowly she climbed back up the bird-filled cliff.

"Come on everybody. Down to the dock!" She heard Bibbi shout.

Reaching the top, Didda spotted the boat a little way out. White froth sprayed out like wings at the bow as the boat swooped up and down in the choppy water. Leaping to her feet, she ran to catch up with her uncle, Grandma and her summer help, Elsa. All of them whooping and running as they headed down to the dilapidated dock.

The pilings were old, barnacle covered, and rotting in places, but still strong enough to hold them as they ran. The wet uneven planks bounced up and down by their clomping feet and made a small bait-bucket rattle. A tattered old fish-net shook as Bibbi ran, then tossed to Grandpa the end of a coiled up rope fastened to an old motor rusting away on the dock.

Catching the rope with his right hand, Grandpa's gnarled left hand held tight on the wheel as he brought the rocking boat to the dock with experienced ease. They started to unload the large, heavy bags of flour, sugar and other supplies, and as always, fighting off the screeching, greedy diving seagulls.

Grandpa was safe, Didda grinned.

CHAPTER 14

Cows Go Crazy in the Spring

It was a sunny day for a change. A rare, warm breeze was blowing from the ocean, causing the salty air to bring faint smell of musty algae and spring weeds. Bibbi was ready to let the cows out for the first time this year. Old Red, Hilda, and the heifer, Freyja, were two-stepping in their stalls. Didda stood outside with her three cousins from the next farm. Nonni, was twelve. His given name was Jonas, but there were so many 'Jonases' already in the family that he was nicknamed Nonni. He had sky-blue eyes that sparkled with mischief, and he was adventurous and outgoing. His sister, Dora, was cautious and timid, while the younger sister, Sina, was a bit of each - cautious and spontaneous.

Didda's Grandpa called them The Three Golden Gremlins, because all had almost identical hair-color; golden yellow, and where ever you saw one, you saw the other two.

"All right, come in and get ready." Bibbi hollered from inside the cow-house.

"I… I don't want to do this, I…I just want to watch." Dora stuttered, cringing.

"Okay, Nonni, you can have Hilda. Sina, you take Freyja, and Diddamin you take Old Red, you know her and her mean ways." Bibbi chuckled.

Just outside the front door, Great-grandma was sitting on a three-legged stool. Grandma Sigrid was perched on the hitching rock. Elsa stood by, arms akimbo, eyebrows knit in a heavy frown. The show was about to begin. The one who held their cows' tail the longest was the winner. Nonni, Sina and Didda had stationed themselves behind their respective cow, firmly grabbing a tail. The cows mooed and twisted their head back to look at kids, and at the same time trying to swing their tail. Old Red was getting riled, her hind feet started stomping from side to side.

"Hurry! Open the door!" Didda jumped away from a hoof aimed at her legs.

"I have to untie them. Dad will open the door when I yell." Bibbi scrambled by the hay-trough, lifting the ropes off the cows' heads.

"Okay, Dad." Bibbi shouted. The door opened, screeching and creaking, having not been opened all winter.

Suddenly, it was as if a fox had jumped into the cow-house. The cows backed out every which-way trying to get outside and at the same time feeling the pull the kids had on their tails. Sina was tugging Freyja's tail, screaming, and urging the heifer to move. Nonni was next, with Hilda dragging him at a fast run, his long skinny legs pumping wildly up and down. His shouting and yelling startled the heifer, which scrambled outside and yanked Sina off her feet. She let go off the tail and Freyja took off jumping and bucking.

Old Red rolled her eyes at Didda and viciously kicked back. Turning as if she was a teen-cow, she took off out of the cow-house at a clumsy kick-hopping clop as the adults laughed and egged them on. Bibbi was whooping like a cowboy herding cattle. Didda glanced sidewise and knew Sina had let go and the heifer was clomping into the field. Didda saw that Nonni was almost catching up with her. She was distracted for a brief moment, but it was enough to cause her to trip and fall on her stomach. She bit into gritty dust but held on as Old Red dragged her on the ground. The cow was kicking and bucking like a bad-mannered horse.

Didda's mouth was getting full of dirt and grass, mixed with blood from a split lip, but she was not about to let go.

"Stop, you've won! Let go, let go" Everyone was screaming at the same time.

Her fingers were frozen in a stubborn death grip as sharp lava pebbles stung her cheeks. Old Red did a turn-around and Didda swung in a big arch. She let go of the tail and tumbled into the creek where they did laundry and washed the wool after the sheep were shorn. She sat in the ice-cold water, her steaming-hot temper at a full boil. She was a bloody, dirty mess. Old Red has gotten the best of her, now the cow was looking at her, rolling her big brown eyes. Didda thought it looked like Old Red was smirking.

Infuriated, Didda watched as the Old REd ambled after the other cows, stopping now and then to curl her long tongue around little tufts of grass. I don't mind a horse dumping me, but a cow, she thought. The whole family came running, hysterically laughing, although the two grandmas were concerned. Bibbi jumped into the creek with a rag in his hand and proceeded to mop off the blood off her face as he pulled her up to her feet.

"She's fine, just madder than a wet hen," Bibbi chortled, as Didda spit out a sliver of lava-shale.

"You'd be mad too if a cow dumped you into the creek!" Didda spat out the words as she glared at her uncle, who kept dabbing at her face, grinning.

"You should have let go." Nonni wiped tears from his eyes with the back of his left hand while still doubled up with laughter.

"Yeah, why didn't you just let go?" Sina and Dora giggled.

Didda started shivering, and then mumbled, "Just get me out of here."

"Here, Bibbi, wrap her up in my shawl." Grandma Sigrid handed him her black wool wrap. As they walked back to the house, Didda's sheepskin shoes made slushy, squeaky sound in harmony with the slop-slop of Bibbi's water filled, sealskin boots. She turned and looked grimly at Old Red, who was totally oblivious of her, contently chewing her cud.

With much merriment, they all got to the farmhouse where Elsa suddenly jumped out the door. Looking at Didda's scratched-up face, she exclaimed. "Good heavens, girl don't you ever learn?" She softened her words by giving Didda a soft thump on the shoulder. "Come on, Diddamin let's get you some hot drink."

After a hot cup of coffee and some cookies Didda got her humor back, she laughed along with the others as each one took a turn in describing the event, each one trying to out-do the other, laughing and slapping their knees.

"I think you are all just plumb crazy." Dora muttered. "I thought you all were going to get killed. That old cow, Red, with her sharp, pointy horns and mean eyes, is the most wicked-looking thing,"

"Well, the old 'thing' doesn't have the best temper in the ruminant world, but her horns sure are beauties." Grandpa stopped a dreamy look. Didda thought he might be thinking of a new snuff-horn. Old Red did have striking markings of black-brown streaks on ivory bone. Those horns would make very handsome tobacco-holders, and would likely could be the envy of the local farmers who competed for the most ornate "snuffy"

"Well now," he continued, "tomorrow we'll start shearing the sheep before turning them out." Rubbing his chin, he squinted at the three towheads. "You, Gremlins want to come over for some work and fun? We'll have eighteen ewes and four rams to shear, also a few lambs to ear-mark."

"Don't forget we'll also be washing the wool in the creek." Grandma motioned to the kids with her cup of coffee.

"We'd love to help." Enthusiastic Nonni spoke also for his two sisters as they nodded. "We'll be back in the morning then."

Waving and hollering "Bless, bless," they headed out the door.

CHAPTER 15

Shearing Time

The next morning they were gathered by the fast running, gurgling creek where Didda had been dumped by Old Red. The sun was shining but not very bright or very warm. It seemed to be lurking behind the thin, raggedy clouds. Didda hoped for the sheep's sake that it would warm up. They were sure to feel cold when their wooly coats were shorn off.The fire was roaring, devouring the dry peat-and-cow chips. Steam from the iron kettle curled up into the cool air and grey-white mist swirled over the bubbles rolling in the water. Elsa dropped in a handful of homemade green lye soap. The effect was like the gushing of a little Geyser shooting up in the air.

Elsa and Grandma were sitting on lava rocks, softly cushioned by thick, silver-grey moss. Great-grandma and Dora were sitting on wood stools just outside the sheepcote, carefully situated to be out of the way when the door would swing open and Bibbi, Grandpa and Nonni would come out with a sheep, hands firmly gripping the horns. Sina and Didda stood by with shears in hand, like nurses in an operating room, knife – scalpel – scissors. The men came out, each one straddling a sheep. When Grandpa stumbled and let go of the ewe, Sina managed to grab a handful stringy, dirty wool slowing the sheep down enough for Didda to grab the horns and frantically hold on. Swinging her leg over the squirming back, she squeezed the ewe between her legs and dug her heels into the ground.

Sina let go as Grandpa grabbed the shears from her hand and took over the horns, twisting the sheep's head to one side and forcing her to lie down. Didda sat down by the ewe's head and held her tight. She kicked her feet a bit and let out a plaintive 'bah.' Grandpa was quick and with his skill, had the sheep shorn quickly. Didda released her, and she shook her head and body vigorously. Didda wondered if the sheep felt as ridiculous as she looked; skinny body, skinny legs, skinny head!

Grandpa went inside to get the next one. Nonni finished shearing his sheep, and Sina let go of the one she had been holding for him.

"Yow, get the ram" Didda heard Bibbi yell in a weird voice

The ludicrous-looking, half-shorn ram was wriggling and clumsily clomping down the field, his feet tangling up in in the wool dragging on the ground. Bibbi was crouched on the ground grabbing his crotch trying to get his breath back. Everyone else tore after ram, formed a circle, and slowly forced the ram to get back to the sheepcote. Bibbi was staggering to his feet, slaughter in his eyes. He seemed all right. Didda didn't dare ask *who is madder than a wet hen now?*

After that, the searing was completed swiftly, and then, it was time to mark the lambs. Didda felt sorry for them as Grandpa cut the two V-marks in their left ear. Dora and Sina averted their eyes as the bright-red blood trickled down and stained the lambs' curly wool. The girls knew that farmers had to mark their sheep but wished there was an easier way. With relief, they heard Elsa shout that the hot water was ready. Gathering up armful of dirty wool, they pitched into the boiling water.

Using long-handled wood poles, Grandpa and Bibbi stirred and then lifted the heavy wet fleece out of the black kettle and into the sparkling clear creek. Didda and her cousins jumped into the ice-cold water and rinsed out any residue of soap, then all worked to spread the wool on the ground to dry. Later on, they gathered the wool and brought it inside.

The dried wool was kept a corner of the kitchen where Grandma had her spinning wheel. A skein of brown was looped over the spindle. Above the spinning wheel was a wood shelf with a clutter of books, and a collection of snuff-horns displayed among the volumes. An oil lamp sat in the middle of the table with its chimney clean and shiny from Elsa's obsessive washing.

Great-Amma would take the skein off the spinning wheel and draped the loop over Didda's hands, who spread them apart so the loop would not droop as Great-Amma started to wind the yarn into a ball. As days went by, Grandma, Elsa and Didda would comb the new wool, while Great-Amma would spin it into desired thickness. Icelandic sheep have an inner, fine undercoat and a coarser outer-coat.

The women knitted the soft Lopi sweaters from the soft inner fleece that Great-Amma just barely spun - this method was called 'lopi'. She spun the outer wool into tight, strong yarn from which they knitted mittens, socks and 'leppar'. Leppar is an innersole for their sheep-skin shoes, and making those was usually the children's first knitting projects. Spinning wheels, combs and looms were a necessary part of Grandma's household equipment.

CHAPTER 16

Grandpa Hires Summer Help

The hustle and the bustle when Grandpa got ready to hire summer help was nothing short of amazing. Didda was shooed from one corner to another while Grandma and Elsa swept, scrubbed, and cleaned.

Green coffee beans were browning in a black kettle that hung over the fire in the fireplace and the strong aroma permeated the kitchen. Didda loved the smell of coffee, and one of her favorite chores was to grind the roasted beans in the wooden coffee mill. When she was set to the task, every so often, she would pull out the boxy drawer at the bottom of the mill and blissfully sniff deeply, as the coffee accumulated. She would watch as Grandma filled the chipped blue and white speckled coffeepot with boiling water. Then, Grandma would drop in a handful of coffee and a pinch of chicory and the water in the pot erupted, hissing and steaming, like a miniature erupting volcano.

A large pot was always cooking away on the back burner of the kitchen stove. Delicious whiffs of the mutton soup that was simmering made Didda's mouth water. All day, bits of mutton-meat, potato, carrots and rutabagas were added. Coffee and soup simmering away all day was a tradition with Grandma.

"Diddamin, we are almost out of sand to scrub the floor with." Grandma said, handing her a grey, beat-up metal bucket. "Run down to the beach and get some. And get the dogs to chase the sheep off the roof."

Didda looked at the floor that, to her, was clean enough to eat off. The planks were as white as could be from numerous down-on-their-knees scrubbing with rough scoria. But, if Grandma says it needs scrubbing, well then, it needs scrubbing. Didda ran across the rock-scattered field and scrambled down the lava cliff, deliberately making scraping racket with the bucket just to startle the starchy, important acting puffins. They seemed so unflappable. She wondered how it would feel to be a puffin, or a seagull, or a kria, just floating ever so smoothly up in the air, without a care. Then here come humans, messing up their lives. Didda felt a slight twinge of remorse: She did not like having her life messed up every spring and every fall. She had traveled from Reykjavik to Vopnafjordur and back again as long as she could remember. She loved the fjord and did not like to have to go back to the city. *I can go to school here just as well*, she thought as she slammed the bucket against the rocks driving hundreds of seagulls into the air, screaming fiercely. They dove at her in a fit of temper before settling back on the lichen and moss covered lava ledges.

Filling the bucket with volcanic sand, Didda stood for a moment watching the hypnotic slow-moving blue-green waves slapping against the glistening-wet black rocks. Long strings of yellow-brown algae floated slowly, up and down, up and down, up and down.

"Hallo, child. What's keeping you?" Elsa leaned precariously over the edge, her shrill voice echoed and bounced off the cliffs causing the seagulls again to fly off into the air, screeching manically.

"I'm coming, I'm coming," Didda grumbled.

"I declare, you're the most day dreaming child I've ever met." She yelled in an aggravated voice. As soon as Didda scrambled back up the cliff, Elsa grabbed the bucket from her hand and ran toward the house shouting, "Don't forget the sheep, your Grandma wants them off the roof before company comes."

Didda got the dogs to chase the protesting sheep off the turf-roof and ran inside. Quietly slipping past the busy women, she sped up the rickety stairs to her favorite place in the whole wide world, Grandpa's attic. The area had an aroma all of its own, musty papers, old leather and tobacco. Even the salty, tangy smell of the ocean found its way into the attic room.

Grandpa had literally hundreds of books lined floor to ceiling, wall to wall, heaped on a table, on top of his massive desk, and stacked on the windowsill. Didda could not walk in a straight line in the room but had to meander around books and old, yellowing newspapers with curled up edges and piled up on the floor in a haphazard manner. She had once asked her Grandpa why he had saved all those old papers, many written in English, she knew he was uncomfortable speaking the language but read it with ease.

"I read about families, like your Grandma's sister, who emigrated to Manitoba, Canada. She, her family, and many others left after the terrible volcano eruption here in Iceland. The Laki eruption in 1784 ruined most of the countryside and for years made living extremely difficult." As Grandpa picked up a paper, fine dust flittered to the floor.

"This here is called *The Heimskringlan,* or *Around The World,* printed in Winnipeg. It is written in Icelandic and tells where some of the Icelanders settled, many on an island called Gimli, in Manitoba. All of these books and papers are like good friends. I read and enjoy them again and again; I wouldn't part with any of them." He fondly patted the stack of papers.

This was pure heaven for the bookworm that Didda was. The stories of the Vikings came to life for her as she and Grandpa had some lively discussions about them - their travels, discoveries, and so-called murderous bloodthirsty ways. She knew that many Vikings were actually farmers. They were also skilled navigators and sailors. Didda knew that an Icelander named Leif Eriksson actually discovered America five hundred years before Columbus.

"Child, come down here." Elsa's thunderous voice shattered Didda's solitude. Sometimes she thought Elsa had eyes in the back of her head. Didda should have known that Elsa saw her slip upstairs.

"I have to brush your hair before company arrives." Elsa shouted as she thumped the wood ceiling.

Fuming, Didda scrambled to her feet. At ten years old, she could brush and braid her own hair without help. The books on the floor bounced as Elsa thumped again, harder this time. Didda did not mess around but flew downstairs and jumped on the three-legged stool that waiting for her. Didda's hazel eyes watered as Elsa undid the long braids and firmly brushed out the tangles. Grimacing and pursing her lips, she gave Didda a no-nonsense look as her ample bosom bobbed up and down with each stroke.

Grandma, who was short and slim, sat on a stool that Grandpa had built just for her. She sat with the butter-churn firmly held in place by her skinny knees. Her black skirt and long white apron hiked up revealed black, wool stockings. She had both hands clamped on the wood butter-pole, hand over hand. The churn slurped and sloshed as

Grandma energetically pumped up and down, making the sleeves on her blouse flop and flounce.

Great-Amma sat in the corner rocking back and forth and knitting so fast that Didda could not see the points of the four, clicking needles. The metal needles made fascinating click-clack rhythm sound as the sock she was knitting took shape.

"Why are you knitting so fast, Great-Amma?" Didda's eyes tried to follow the blur of needles.

Finishing a row, she pulled out one needle and used it to push an escaping tuft of white hair back under the black cap she always wore. The cap had a long tassel, reaching from her left ear down past her shoulder, a carved three-inch silver cylinder placed close to the cap kept the long strands form separating. Like Grandma and Elsa, she wore a long skirt and an apron tied at the waist.

She had on a black vest intricately embroidered with silver thread, and laced up at the front with a silver chain that hung over her bosom. The vest was similar to the other women's Sunday clothes but Great-Amma wore dress-ups every day, except during haying time when the men cut the grass near the farm, at which time she would put on a knit sweater, then kind of waddle out to help rake and turn the rows of hay.

Scratching her head with the point of the needle, she quizzically looked at Didda. She had a habit of cocking her head to one side and closing her left, blue eye, while wide-opening her right, brown eye.

"I want to get this sock done before I run out of yarn." Grinning, she held up a slowly disappearing ball then looked up into the faces of chuckling Grandma and Elsa.

"Great-Amma, you're teasing me, it's the same amount of yarn whether she knitted fast or slow." Didda got off the stool in a huff and went to look for Grandpa. She could hear him in the guest room, blowing his nose. A rake was lying on the floor across the doorway bending down she picked it up and leaned it against the wall.

"You're hired." Grandpa's voice boomed.

She jumped. "What? Oh, Grandpa, I bet you could be heard all the way outside!"

"Diddamin, I've taught you right." Grandpa gleefully slapped and rubbed wrinkled, red hands on his knees. "I'm getting ready to hire summer workers and I laid the rake there as a test. If a person steps over it, I will not hire them. The same goes if they kick it aside, but if they do what you just did, it is an indication of a good worker. I learned that from my Father who learned it from his father. It has worked well for us for generations." He chuckled and blew his nose again.

"Oh, Grandpa, you are funny." She giggled.

Grandpa had very thick, black hair now peppered with gray. Bushy eyebrows over keen, dark-brown eyes and a handlebar, greying mustache that he had a habit of twirling when meditating, or working on endless math-problems. Besides reading, he had a passion for math. Papers, scribbled with fraction problems were scattered about wherever he rested for a bit. Didda thought that was strange, she did not like math at all.

"I heard the butter-churn sloshing, and now I smell fresh-baked bread." Grandpa scrunched his nose, sniffed, tilted his head back and roared. "How about some coffee and fresh bread, Elsa?"

Grandma's blue figurine-painted china was already on the table, covered with a handsomely embroidered white tablecloth that she had decorated in an intricate cutout design. Grandma always put out her best for company. Visitors were rare in this rugged, remote fjord.

Elsa brought in the coffee, along with the scrumptious hot brad and a bowl of butter. Grandpa poured part of his coffee into the cup's saucer then held the small dish between his hands and blew on the drink to cool, and then he took a sip. Didda watched him for a moment then imitated him. Grandpa grinned as he reached over and tore off two thick pieces of the hot bread and smeared on big slabs of butter that melted and ran down the sides and onto the dish.

They sat by the window and looked at the mountain bathed in rare rays of golden-red light, and made the blue-green ocean glimmer and shimmer. Didda saw their reflection in the glass. As did Grandpa. His eyes crinkled at the corners as he smiled at her, nodding his head reading her mind.

"Diddamin, there's no place like this." He said softly.

Contently sipping her coffee from the china cup and looking at their reflections in the window glass, she whole-heartedly agreed. She wanted to stay here, like this, forever.

She heard the yipping of dogs, neighing of horses and cheery greetings.

Company had arrived.

CHAPTER 17

Hanna

Didda ran outside in time to see Helgi, whom she had met last year, dismount and grab Bibbi in a bear hug.

"Good to see you, Helgi" Bibbi suddenly stopped, staring at Helgi's companion. Didda was surprised that her normally glib uncle seemed at a loss for words.

Looking back at Helgi he asked somewhat haltingly, "Is this your cousin you said wanted to work for Dad this summer?"

Bibbi's eyes were glued on the young lady as she swung her legs gracefully off of her horse, a lazy looking cross-eyed roan. The young woman looked about eighteen, and was very attractive. She wore loose fitting long trousers that looked more like a split skirt and a white sweater with an intricate Icelandic knit pattern. In her right hand, she held a whip with an elaborately designed silver handle.

Her blond hair was in braids that wound around on top of her head like a golden crown that almost gave her an ethereal appearance. She had wide, violet-blue eyes that did not miss much, like the admiring look from Bibbi.

She gave Didda a slow right-eye wink that reminded her of Sunna. Didda loved her right away and tried to figure out how she could give this young woman a hint about Grandpa's test. She could not think of anything, but fervently hoped that this delightful newcomer would pick up the rake before she entered the guest-room.

"Welcome, Jóhanna, come on in." Grandpa called.

"Blessings on your home." Jóhanna smiled and started to step inside. Stopping, she reached down, picked up the rake, and leaned it carefully against the wall. She stood up and greeted Grandpa.

"Glad to meet you, Björn Jónasson. Please call me Hanna, my mother is Jóhanna." As they shook hands, Didda, grinning from ear to ear, peeked around Hanna and caught Grandpa's face. She knew they had new help.

Turning around, she almost tripped over Bibbi's feet. He and Helgi had followed close behind them, Bibbi unable to take his eyes off the girl. Didda noticed Helgi was watching Bibbi, an oddly sad smile curving his lips. She thought about that for a moment then shook her head I'm letting my silly imagination run wild again!

Grandpa shook hands with Helgi and motioned for the couple to sit down. Bibbi sat down where he had good view of Hanna.

"Diddamin, ask Elsa to bring us some more bread and coffee." Grandpa said with humorous glint in his eyes as he observed Bibbi's reaction to the girl. Didda thought Grandpa himself was acting a little strange. He usually tilted his head back in the chair and bellowed for his coffee. Now, he was quite the gentleman. She went to speak with Elsa.

As the adult visited, Didda watched Helgi's cousin with curiosity, especially because of Bibbi's obvious interest. Her uncle was an accomplished accordion player and was much sought after to play at weddings, country-dances in nearby villages and out-door gatherings like the fall sheep-roundup. With his quick, mischievous smile, bright blue eyes, auburn hair and broad shoulders he was very popular with the young ladies, but hadn't been particularly interested in any of them. Didda had always thought of him as an adult, but now he became just as goofy as the boys at school who liked to yank her braids. Hanna didn't seem interested in Bibbi. Her soft, serene glance was the same for all of them. Grandpa told Hanna she was hired, and shortly after Helgi took off for his family farm.

Didda was old enough to help the adults with the haying but had a hard time keeping up with Hanna, who was a whirlwind of a worker. Furiously raking the rows of hay, Hanna caused the grass to whirl up as in a strong, northern gale. Every so often she'd lean over and take a strange gulping breath. Didda thought she was working too hard and wanted to tell her Grandpa, but Hanna gave her a warning look as she shook her head and put a finger to her lip then went back to raking with intense determination. Grandpa's test was good.

CHAPTER 18

Do Dogs and Horses Have 'ESP'?

"**A**ren't you ready to go? They are almost here and we will miss the tide if we don't hurry." Didda shouted to Hanna, who was still inside the house.

Standing outside, she watched her three girlfriends from nearby farmsteads as they arrived. Gréta, and Sína were both ten, and Unnur, Sína sister was eleven. They were gleefully laughing as their horses came across the field, manes and tails flying.

"Hi, should we dismount?" Unnur asked, as her horse came to a hoof-rearing stop.

"Hi all." Didda waved. "No, I don't think you need to. I just hollered for Hanna, and she should be right out." She finished adjusting the stirrups on her saddle as she saw Hanna in the doorway. They were going swimming in a geothermal-warm swim hole on the other side of the fjord's inlet and Hanna was planning to ride Thunder for the trip. Her cross-eyed horse was getting old and stayed pretty much out in the pasture until needed at haying time.

Hanna stepped outside and walked up to Thunder who nervously shied away from her. Her hair was in two long braids and hung almost to her waist. Swinging her right braid over her shoulder, she tipped her head, puzzled. Their horses snorted, impatiently chewed at the bits, and pranced about. All the horses except Bibbi's horse, Thunder, who was almost subdued. Hanna worked to saddle Thunder and the horse remained passive.

Didda had never seen him like this. Thunder was well known for his competitive nature, and could not stand to have another horse in front of him. He was the fastest runner in their county, and Bibbi proudly displayed several of their racing awards in his room.

Didda hoped Thunder wasn't sick. Darting inside she called for Bibbi. He and Grandpa were at the kitchen table drinking coffee.

"Would you both come out and look at Thunder? He's not acting like himself." Didda said as unease churning in her stomach.

Bibbi shot up out of his seat. The chair teetered for a moment before tumbling over and skittering on the wood floor. Both he and Grandpa ran outside. Carefully, they ran their hands over the horse, looked into his eyes, and checked his mouth. Grandpa examined Hanna's saddle thoroughly. Thunder tossed his head at the close inspection. Now switching his tail, he nuzzled Bibbi then started his usual prancing around eager for a run; he sure seemed to have recovered very quickly. Didda calmed her own horse who was getting restless.

"This is the first time Thunder has acted like he doesn't like me to saddle him or even like me at all." She murmured.

"I'll just take him for a quick run and see how he does." Bibbi jumped into Hanna's saddle. The stirrups were too short, but he managed to scrunch up his legs and take off at a brisk gallop across the field. Thunder went into his well-known tolt and from there into 'flying pace'. The flying pace is unique to Icelandic horses, where the horse moves both legs of one side at the same time. Bibbi and his horse became as one in a spectacular flying form. Thunder's bronze coat with the black mane glistened in the sun, his black tail plumed out behind him and his four black socks were a blur.

"Not a thing wrong with that horse." Grandpa proclaimed proudly. Thunder was born on grandpa's farm when Bibbi was twelve. His dad had given him the colt with the understanding that Bibbi would have complete charge both in caring for and training him. Bibbi had done an outstanding job and Grandpa was justifiably proud of both his son and the horse.

"Thunder is fine, Hanna." Bibbi swung off of Thunder, who was breathing loudly." He is just a little temperamental when I am not the one in the saddle. I guess I have him a little spoiled. It will do him good to get used to you."

With much excitement and laughter, the girls took off. All the way to the inlet, Thunder stayed behind the other horses. This was so unusual that Didda could not help but to look back. Thunder was staying behind the horses. It was unbelievable. A strange foreboding crept down Didda's spine. The three girls had already entered the inlet, giggling as the cold water sprayed over their legs. Star, Didda's horse, was just going in when she heard Hanna's voice.

"Come up here, old boy." Patting the back of her saddle as Bibbi and Grandpa had often done before for the old dog.

Blackie whimpered and stuck his tail between his legs. To Didda's astonishment, the old dog took a flying leap and landed on Star, right behind her.

Didda looked at Hanna, and her face was ashen. She looked like she had seen a ghost.

"What's the matter, Hanna?" Didda whispered, looking around, scared. Did we disturb hidden folks? Did Hanna see a tröll hiding behind a rock?

Nothing had bothered the three horses ahead of them as they plodded ahead, sloshing great deal of water as they went across the bay.

"It's nothing. I just felt funny for a minute. I think Thunder and Blackie have me spooked!" Her laugh sounded a little forced.

"Maybe we should wait to go swimming, Hanna." Didda thought Hanna looked quite ill.

All of a sudden, Thunder decided it was time to move. Wading in, he took off more like his old self and almost galloped into the water. Star followed at a sedate pace. Didda heard the girls' laughter and the pounding hoofs as the horses got out of the bay and onto dry ground then taking off at a brisk canter. Thunder and Star sloshed across the inlet and reached the dry ground, where both horses acted as if it was time to race, but Star a sure loser.

Didda did not understand the animal's behavior. It was so unusual. The sun was shining between puffy clouds that were lazily floating in the pale-blue sky. Racing to the pool, the girls tore off their clothes down to their underwear, and flung themselves in. There was a big splash and gleeful shrieking as they jumped up and down in the naturally warm waterhole.

Hanna, being the adult, tried to slow the girls down without much success. The water was just right and the four younger girls were having a glorious time; this was the only naturally warm waterhole for miles around.

Shivering, Unnur and Sina got out and wrapped themselves in towels. Gréta and Didda started to pull themselves out when Unnur pointed to the water.

"Hanna is on the bottom, something is wrong with her!" She shrieked as she pointed.

Didda saw Hanna, face down in the water.

The way she was laying so still, Didda knew she was not pulling a prank. That was not like Hanna anyway. She felt Greta dive down alongside her and pulled Hanna to the surface. Hanna was deathly white and her wide-open eyes were completely blank. Her braids had come loose and her golden hair floated about her face.

Didda screamed. Once she started, she found she couldn not stop.

As in a nightmare, she heard Greta yell "Quick Sina, quick! Ride up to the farm there and get Jon! Unnur help us lift Hanna out!"

Hanna's body was a dead weight and proved to be more than the girls could manage. They were all crying and sobbing as they tried to keep Hanna's head out of the water until help arrived.

Sina was back from the nearby farm in moments with Jon. He waded into the water and gently took the burden from them.

"I should have known something was wrong. It's my fault." Didda wailed. "Thunder and Blackie knew something was wrong. I should have known." Her teeth chattered as she rocked back and forth, rubbing her eyes with her fists.

"No, it wasn't anyone's fault." Jon's voice was comforting. "I know Hanna's family. We have all known since she was a baby she has had a heart condition. She never want to be treated differently than any other kid. She was not expected to live past her thirteenth birthday." He patted Didda's shoulder. "This is very sad, but she lived her life the way she wanted to."

The sober, still-shocked group slowly gathered around Hanna and waited. The family came and took over, they tried to console the girls but there was just so much to do. Jon took the girls to their respective homes. They mounted their horses, and Didda buried her face in Star's mane. Unnur stared, dry-eyed, straight ahead. Sina and Greta wept, tears streaming down their cheeks.

Jon and his wife rode with them. At each farm, the couple quietly spoke with the families of the girls. Grandpa's farm was the last stop and Jon's horse galloped ahead. In one motion, he swung off his horse and dashed inside. Grandpa came running out and grabbed Didda off of Star and held her tight as he whispered, "Hush now, it's going to be alright."

She stopped sobbing, feeling numb.

As they came in, Bibbi was standing by the door, stone-faced. He looked into Didda's tear-stained face, and then grabbed her in a fierce hug before bolting out the door. She heard Thunder's hoofs as he galloped away.

"If we'd just not gone swimming, or if I'd listened to Thunder, maybe this would not have happened. I knew something was wrong and I did not do anything. It's my fault." Didda stuttered.

"Come here, Diddamin." Grandma wrapped her arms around sobbing Didda and led her to Great-grandma, who was in her rocking chair, lifting Didda unto her lap.

"She was too young and pretty to die. I should have been able to save her." Didda started wailing again.

"Hush now, child. You heard what Jon said about her having heart problems since with her hankie, was born. None of you, none of us could have done anything to save her life."

Great-grandma rubbed and patted Didda's back, as she dabbed at her own eyes with her hankie. She continued softly, "Hanna was doing what she wanted to do, to be like all the other girls, as long as she could. You know she worked as hard, or harder, than many others just to prove to herself she could. She'd like for you to remember how she enjoyed life."

The soothing rocking and her singsong murmuring relaxed Didda so that she began to of Hanna. The more she thought, the more she remembered the way Hanna had lived and the numerous times she mentioned God and His angels, even guardian angels, which Didda thought might be a good thing to have. Didda decided she would be more like Hanna. She was not sure if she could do it because Hanna was so good and Didda tended to get herself into hot water quite often. Didda went to sleep and did not even know when she was carried off to bed.

The next morning it was almost warm, for late August. Nonni, Unnur, Sina and Didda sat halfway up on the turf roof of the sheepcote.

"I'm going to miss you when you go back to Reykjavik next week." Unnur said, squinting at Didda with moist eyes

"I'd like to go to school in the city." Nonni muttered, as he chewed on a blade of grass he had stuck between his teeth. Sina did not say a word. Her head was bent as she worked her fingers around a small tuft of grass.

"Well, I don't want to go, I like it here. I'd like to stay forever." Didda said, grumpily.

For a while, they sat without speaking, Didda gazed over the farm and ocean. On the horizon, a ship was making its way north across the mouth of the fjord, a plume of black smoke trailed in the air. It looks like a trawler that was not stopping in their fjord.

"I hope they had enough pins to protect Hanna." Nonni sat up abruptly. "She was too nice to turn into a ghost."

Didda looked at him, stunned His sisters turned to him, mouths open and stared bug-eyed at their brother. Nonni turned beet-red at their reaction. "You know what I'm talking about, how you have to put pins into a dead person's shoes to help them from turning into ghosts." He said defensively.

"Great-Amma said that Hanna was in heaven so she couldn't have turned into a ghost." Didda pointed her finger into his face so menacingly that he jerked back. "She also had a guardian angel to protect her. She did not need pins. When I get older, I am going to ask God for one of those angels. Maybe Hanna was so good because those angels kept her out of trouble."

The sisters nodded, agreeing with Didda, but Nonni looked troubled. "Boys are supposed to be strong. I guess angels are alright to help girls, but I can take care of myself!" He looked at them defiantly as he stood up and brushed his pants.

CHAPTER 19

Surprise in the Net

"Hey, Didda, want to go fishing? Dad says we can take our skiff." Nonni bellowed as he and the girls came across the field, each one carrying fish buckets and pole.

"Sure, wait, I'll get my stuff." Didda ran inside, but stuck her head out right away. "Grandma wants to know if you have snack-food with you. Oh, never mind she's already got some stuff in my bucket." Didda laughed.

Didda caught up and the four went running down to the rickety dock and to their father's boat, tied up alongside her Grandpa's boat. Jumping aboard, Nonni caused the boat to rock violently. They had to grab the tiller to keep from falling into the ocean. Unnur and Didda giggled.

"Served you right if you'd gotten soaking wet." Unnur laughed. "Remember what Dad's always telling you." She changed her girlish voice into a deep growl. "Now, son, you've got to slow down and learn to look before you leap." Then she doubled up with laughter, but Sina frowned.

"All right, all right." Nonni mumbled. "Hand me the poles." He put the poles on top of the oars, which was lying on the bottom of the skiff along with a net. Didda and Unnur followed with their buckets in hand, but Sina did not move.

"I don't want to go, I'll wait here. You all put on the life-jackets." She said in a motherly voice.

Smiling, the three pulled out three bright-yellow jackets from the hold and put them on Nonni pulled the cord on the outboard motor, which kicked into start immediately.

"Motor sounds really good," Didda exclaimed.

"Well, the boat is old, but the motor is new." Nonni smiled, expertly handling the tiller.

Waving at Sina, he steered the boat toward middle of the bay. The skiff was low enough for Didda and Unnur to have their fingers playing in the ice-cold ocean, yelping as spray splashed on their face.

"Unnur, let's throw the net over the side and see if we catch something interesting."

Didda bent down and pulled on one end of the small net. She fastened one end on a peg at the bow and threw the rest overboard. The net opened and started trailing alongside the skiff.

"Hey, that trawler is causing some great waves. Whoo-hoo, we're in its wake. Hold on the waves are building up." Nonni steered the skiff into a big, undulating bulge coming their way

"The ship has disturbed some harbor seals, a big one is right here. Oh no - a baby one is under us." Unnur screamed.

Suddenly the boat lifted up, and Nonni was catapulted backward, hitting his head hard on the oar. Didda reached over and turned off the motor. The boat slowed down and veered closer to where the larger seal was. The little seal was nowhere in sight. Rubbing his head, Nonni looked up and noticed the tightness of the net, as if it were full of fish.

"Pull up the net, I think we have us some good catch. That big seal looks he is eying our fish." Nonni sat up.

Getting over their first panic-attack, the girls each grabbed part of the net. Didda and Unnur did their best, pulling as they were grunting and groaning. The boat rocked and dipped as they worked to get the net up. Suddenly, it flew over the side and into the boat. Three good-sized fish were flopping on the bottom of the boat along with something brown and about three-foot long.

"Yikes, that's a baby seal" Didda shrieked as she threw her end of the net down.

Nonni saw a small brown head among three fish. "Oh, man yes, it is a baby seal and that is probably the mama."

He paused for a moment, and then grimaced. "Help me throw it back. I sure wouldn't want a shape-shifting mama-seal getting mad at us." The large seal swam closer, large shining eyes watching as Unnur and Nonni lifted the small creature.

"Nonni, you know that's just a folktale. You know there are no shape-shifters" Unnur scoffed.

"Sure is heavy for such a little one." She grunted.

"Folklore? That depends on who you are talking to." Nonni smirked.

Didda listened with much interest then opened her mouth to say something but a hollering from Sina, who was hopping up and down on the pier stopped her.

"We just caught a baby seal, throwing it back to its mama." Unnur yelled.

"Well, look at that, we got three two-foot codfish and a baby seal in one little net. Who is going to believe that fish story?" Didda crowed.

CHAPTER 20

The North Fjords

Summer was over and Didda was on her way back to Reykjavik. Unlike the sleek Godafoss II, this ship, the Gullfoss, was like a heavy-set elderly woman, elbowing herself through a crowd as it plowed through the ocean at full speed toward their first stop.

The sky was a lead grey color. The constant stiff wind-gusts bit Didda's cheeks and the stung her eyes. The tip of her nose was red and ice-cold. Didda tucked her chin deep into the thick collar of her sweater as she sat, hunched up, in the fo'castle, amid coiled-up brown rope and wood crates. She wrapped her arms across her chest as she rocked back and forth. Just a few hours of sailing and already she missed everyone at Vopnafjordur. She did not want to leave. She did not want to go back to Reykjavik.

A whiff of smoke caused her to look up. Two men were standing at the rail. One of them was round and short. The top of his head was covered with a limp black hat. He had a curled-down shiny black pipe clenched between his teeth. The pipe bobbed up rapidly and down as he spoke with both hands jammed into his pockets of his overcoat. The other man was taller. A lanky bareheaded younger man. With his heavy coat unbuttoned, he'd reached inside and looped his left thumb under one strip of his frayed, black suspenders, yanking and snapping them as he used his straight pipe as a pointer. Didda watched as he removed the pipe from his mouth with his right hand and jab it into the air as he made a comment. The smoke odor reminded her of Grandpa and his attic. She squeezed her eyes hard, refusing to let any tears escape.

"Are you alright?" She lifted her head at the concerned voice and the feeling of a hand gently laid her shoulder.

Didda looked up into the dark-brown eyes of the captain, Einar, who had graduated from the Navigator's School with her Dad. She had known him forever. Einar was a father of twins who were a year older than Didda. Right now, she did not want to talk to him. She just wanted to talk to Sunna, who had been so understanding as they traveled the fjords last Spring. Maybe she had answers to the questions that were churning inside of her.

"Yes, thank you." Didda answered politely.

"You are getting pretty wet from the sprays. You look like a lamb that's falling into a creek." He chuckled as he brushed the water off her sweater.

He sounded just like Sara. Didda stood up.

"Why don't you go down below and dry off a bit. We'll be stopping at the next village pretty soon." Looking into his kind face, Didda nodded. Giving her a soft pat on the shoulder, he left.

As she clambered down the metal steps, she saw the back of a woman who slipped into a cabin. Something about the jet-black hair pulled into a tight bun looked familiar, but Didda could not remember where she might have seen this woman before. She had not seen many passengers topside and wondered if they had all gone to bed already or if it was because the ship was like a cork in a puddle. It rolled and wallowed in the slightest of waves.

She shared a cabin with three older, very quiet women. A top berth had rope webbing in front to keep her from rolling when the ship tilted in a wave. The ladies took little notice of her, which suited Didda just fine. They seemed to be overly sensitive to the motion of the ship. It got pretty ripe in there, so Didda stayed topside as much as possible. Moving quickly, Didda pulled her suitcase out. Changing into a dry sweater and pulling off her damp socks, she hung her wet clothes on couple of pegs so they could dry out for another wear.

They were well into the bay of their next stop when Didda came back up on deck. She noticed that the ship had not gone to the dock, instead a tugboat met them and loaded and unloaded what little cargo there was. No one got off and no one got on. She looked at the small wharf and saw it was dilapidated. The tide was low and showed that the pilings were rotted in several places, high out of the water on one side and sagging on the other.

As they sailed back out and around the formidable cliffs of the peninsula, Didda's mouth dropped in awe. There were millions and millions of seabirds filling the over-crowded sheer crags. It was mind-boggling. She could not imagine any birds left in the world. They must all be here on this rock-face! A huge lava-rock column, named Big-Man, stood by itself in the ocean, it was so teeming with Gannets it did not seem possible to squeeze in another feather let alone a whole bird. Yet, they swarmed, dipped and landed, somehow finding a place to squeeze in.

The ship was now sailing in westerly direction close to the Arctic Circle. The constant wind had become calm but felt bitter cold when Didda moved from the shelter. She wrapped her sweater tighter and stared at the unending ocean. On the north horizon, where open sea should have been, there appeared to be a huge land mass. It was a bunch of massive towering icebergs floating east and south in the North-Atlantic Ocean. It was far enough away to be of no danger to the ship, but the air got noticeably colder. They encountered several ice floes as they continued on west.

On one of the slabs, there was a large polar bear and a smaller one. The sight caused terrific excitement and fear among some of the passengers. Didda squinted at the animals. The larger bear was a straw yellow color, not the white that she had expected. The fur of both bears looked bedraggled.

"They look sad and pitiful with their heads hanging down like that." One of the passengers remarked.

"They've probably traveled on that floe broken from those icebergs on the horizon." Einar said, coming alongside where the group gathered by the rail, watching the bears. "It'd be a shame if they try to swim to land. They'd be hunted down immediately." He shook his head, sadly.

"Why would anyone do that?" Didda exclaimed, appalled.

"There aren't any bears in our country and we want to keep it that way." Einar said, his voice husky. "A few, like those two, have drifted on ice close enough to swim ashore, but they were quickly disposed of. Folks here are extremely afraid of them and with good cause. Polar bears are very dangerous, especially when hungry."

Didda was glad to see them float out of sight. She fervently hoped they found a place where they could be safe.

CHAPTER 21

Gunnar and the Polar Bear

The dock at their next stop, Kopasker, was filled with excitement. Didda was standing by the rail when a man came running to Einar. She overheard the man tell him a hunt was on for a polar bear sighted near town. Folks were running and yelling, unable to agree where this animal was or even if there was one.

A thirteen-year old boy named Gunnar had taken his rowboat out into the fjord to do some fishing. He had navigated around an ice floe, which had been stuck half on shore and half in the sea. Gunnar said that as he rowed his boat to the other side of the floe, he saw something move on the ice. As he watched in horror, a bear, bigger than his horse, he said, jumped across the ice and loped up the countryside. Gunnar frantically rowed his boat back to the pier and began and screaming at the top of his lungs. "Polar bear on land, I saw a polar bear on land!"

On board the ship, the captain tried to continue business as usual. The seamen loading and unloading cargo had trouble keeping their focus. They were constantly glancing over their shoulders to watch the activities of the villagers. A loud whooping from of a group of men brought everyone to the rail. A few passengers left the ship and rushed to the knot of people that had gathered. Everyone was jabbering and pointing.

"I'm not sure you should see this. It may be gruesome." Einar said as he stepped onto the pier, Didda right behind him.

Someone moved as Didda walked closer. Through the little opening, she saw what everyone was gaping at, the scene was clear. A huge bear was sprawled on a flat wagon, four paws hanging over the edges. Bright red blood oozed from a hole in the middle of its broad chest. The small unseeing eyes were open and lifeless.

All the agony of Hanna's death surged through her being. She trembled violently from head to toe then turned and ran toward the ship, nausea twisting through her stomach. She did not make it. Halfway on the pier, she had to run to the edge, where she hung onto a reeking fish-barrel. Heaving, she vomited into the ocean, and then pounded her fists on the stinking barrel, totally miserable.

She felt a cold, wet cloth on her face, turning she looked up into Einar's troubled face through tear-blurred eyes.

"It was a magnificent-looking bear, but very dangerous." He said. "It was obviously half-starved and would have attacked livestock or even people. The villagers had to kill him." Einar brushed her hair with his rough hands.

"I know," she gulped. "But it still doesn't seem right. None of this 'dying' stuff is right." Didda retorted, angrily.

He looked at her, puzzled. Reaching with his right hand he pulled her up to her feet just as the whistle blew, preparing the ship for departure.

Dragging her feet, she went below to her cubbyhole of a bed. Tucking her knees up to her chin, she completely covered her head, twisting the blanket into a tight shroud. Why do people have to drown? Why kill the poor hungry bear? Then she remembered - I wanted Grandma to wring the rooster's neck, and that would have killed him. Confused, she fell asleep.

Loud clamoring, running feet and shouting jarred her awake. Peeking out the porthole, she jerked back as an enormous splash of seawater pummeled the glass. Quickly she clambered up the metal steps she heard the thrilled voices of passengers squealing. "Look there's another one! At least a dozen of them. Look!"

The astounding sight that met her eyes wiped out, for the time being, all of her previous misery. The magnificent whales that breached gracefully, even playfully, up and down in the ocean were breathtaking. Their powerful spouts made explosive swoosh shooting up like Geysers. A dolphin shot up and seemed to do a slow twirl in the air. Its beautiful black and white body shone like it was dressed in a slinky, satin tuxedo. Didda watched, mesmerized until most of the whales had swum north and out of sight. She decided to go back below deck to pick out what she wanted to wear when she would meet Sara again.

Hearing the Gullfoss announce their arrival with the usual blasts, Didda rushed up to find a good place at the rail. She leaning over and stared hypnotically down at the sea, watching the ship's wake. She would never get tired of watching moving water.

More and more passengers were now gathered topside. Suitcases and boxes piled close to the gate where the gangplank would be lowered. She found it interesting to see how people dressed for the unpredictable weather. The older folks had only a sweater thrown casually over their shoulders. A few young men had on heavy coats and caps set at a rakish angle, while most of the young girls were bareheaded, their hair blowing freely in the ever-present wind.

Rain-grey clouds hung over the mountain tops, but the dock was dry. A sizable crowd had gathered to meet the Gullfoss. Didda searched the group as they milled about. Then she spotted Sara standing to one side, shielding her eyes with her right hand as she watched the ship ease up to the pier. She had thrown a large, black shawl over her head. With her left hand, she bundled it tightly under her chin. It made her look much older than she was and a little dowdy. When she saw Didda waving and jumping up and down her great smile lit up her face.

"Have you seen that woman, Sara, your Aunt told me about?" Einar had stopped. He carried a thick stack of papers in his left hand that he used to motion at the people on the dock.

"Yes, she's over there. See that lady right in front with the black shawl?" Didda pointed and waved. As Sara waved back, Einar gave her a crisp salute.

"You have about three hours." He cautioned Didda with a smile "I'll check and make sure you are on board before we leave." His brown eyes twinkled as he chuckled and walked away. His measured, purposeful steps so like her father's she felt momentary sense of longing. Her Dad had been out to sea when she left last spring. She did not see him very often.

Amid much shouting and greetings of families reuniting, Didda followed the passengers disembarking. She worked her way to Sara, who had to take few steps back as Didda exuberantly threw herself into Sara's open arms. After hugging and laughing, they walked arm in arm to a nearby oceanfront café. The fancy name did not disguise that it was just a ramshackle, red-rusted corrugated shack that had five round scarred wood tables. A few chairs were scattered with uneven numbers at the tables, as if people had indiscriminately used them and then not bothered to put them back properly.

As they seated themselves, Didda looked around. In one corner, two men were playing Chess, oblivious to all but each other and their chessmen. Four oil-lamps hung from the rough unfinished rafters, their chimneys streaked with black soot. The place reeked of an odd mixture of fish, coffee, tobacco and kerosene.

After ordering coffee and cookies, Sara turned to Didda. "The family I am with need me a little longer so I will not be going to Reykjavik this time." Reaching out she patted Didda's hand. "The girls that I take care of are about your age. They are in Girl Scouts and last weekend I went with their group to Myvatn. They baked bread in the hot ground."

She rummage a bit in the large black bag she carried. Pulling out a tin can, she handed it to Didda. "I had told them about our travel together so they baked this just for you."

"'Tell them thanks when you see them. I wish I could have been with them. Baking bread in the boiling geothermal mud-holes, how cool is that!" Didda smiled wistfully.

Pinching off a piece of the bread, she put it into her mouth and rolled it around her tongue, tasting its sweetness. Unconsciously crumbling a piece between her fingers, she dropped her head, staring at the crumbs on the table. Then she felt Sara watching her, Didda looked up, her friend's eyes crinkled at the corner as she squinted, eyebrows tightly knit, and eyes dark with concern. Her coffee forgotten, she leaned forward and reached out, laying her hands on top of Didda's, squeezing tightly.

"This sad face of yours doesn't have much to do with me not going to Reykjavik, does it?" She asked.

Didda shook her head. "No. Well, maybe a little bit." Her hands trembled.

Sara nodded, waiting.

"Do you remember Ingi, at Seydisfjord, and his ten-year old son, Ragnar, and the real bad storm we had?" Pulling her hand away, she rubbed her face.

"That's something I'll never forget." Sara shivered.

"Did you know they all went down with the ship?" From the shock on Sara's face, Didda knew she had not heard. Suddenly, she just spilled out everything about Hanna and ended up with the awful killing of the bear.

"So why did Ragnar, his Dad and uncles have to drown? Even the bear had not hurt anybody. He was just hungry. It all seems so unfair!" She put her forehead on Sara's hands.

She just wanted to understand, she had been unable to talk about the things that lay so heavy on her heart. Events had moved too fast at Grandpa's and Aunt Thora's. The last patient had left the infirmary two days before she left Vopnafjordur. There seemed to be no time to sit down and really talk, she probably couldn't have anyway, so soon after what happened. She looked up as Sara leaned forward with a serious look on her face

"Listen, Diddamin. We know Ingi was not wise. Other fishermen had quit fishing that day and sailed back into the harbor for safety. Ingi had the same information on the weather as they did, but he chose not to heed the warning. Some people think they are invincible and nothing will happen to them. Many have lost their lives because of their own stubbornness."

She was silent for a moment bowing her head. When she looked up her eyes were misty with unshed tears.

"I met Hanna when she was thirteen." She said, softly.

"You knew Hanna?" Didda said, surprised.

"I met her and her family in the hospital when visiting my younger sister. My sister and Hanna both had the same heart problems. They were just born that way. I was glad to know that Hanna had several wonderful years and I know how much she enjoyed being with you and your family. It's kind of funny that I didn't know the connection with you until last week."

She smiled that big smile of hers. Sara's story completely lifted Didda's spirit. It was really true. She could not have saved Hanna, no matter how hard she had tried. No matter what action she had taken differently. Didda got off her chair, feeling like the huge weight of guilty feelings had rolled off her shoulders. She felt light as a downy feather as she went to Sara and slipped an arm around her neck.

"Thank you, Sara. I'm really sorry about your sister." Didda kissed her cheek as Sara squeezed her tight, nodding. "Deep down, I really understood about the bear, I just overreacted. So will we meet in Reykjavik sometime?" Didda cocked her head, grinning.

"Absolutely, my love." Sara got up and grabbed Didda, whirling her right to the door. The timing was perfect. The blast of the ship's horn let them know it was time to leave. My love, Didda's mind sang over and over as she ran up the gangplank and boarded the ship. Halfway up, she tuned just as Sara turned and blew her a kiss. Didda felt on top of the world as she returned the kiss.

Clutching the bread-tin tightly in her hand, she meandered to the bow of the ship. Scrunching down, she wiggled until she was comfortable between coiled-up rope and folded-up piece of canvas. There always seemed to be plenty of thick rope. The size of her skinny arms, rolled up, fore and aft, making either place a cozy hide-away.

Opening the tin can, she pinched off a lump of the dark rye bread and stuck it in her mouth. Contently chewing, she leaned back and stared up into the sky, watching the clouds rolling and tumbling along. Like the moving of water, the clouds are just fascinating. She pinched off another piece of her mouthwatering bread as she pondered the volcanic hot spot where the Scouts had baked it. She wondered about other countries, were they anything like Iceland? Fire and ice side by side. Boiling mud pools and steaming fumaroles? Volcanic eruptions and earthquakes every few years? She dosed off, unaware of the two seagulls patiently waiting for an opportunity to take off with the rest of her bread.

CHAPTER 22

It's Fishy Out There

As they sailed north from Akureyri, Didda thought about the earth- tremor that had scared her and her sister, Lilla, half to death. She knew the quake had started not far from their next stop. As the Gullfoss plowed her way through the waves, a cloud of seabirds clamored in the air. Didda watched ducks fly up from the water and disappear among the clouds.

As the ship eased up to the pier at Dalvik, it passed a couple of boys sitting in a rowboat, fishing. They look about my age. They waved and she waved back.

After the gangplank lowered, Didda disembarked and picked her way along the dock, around the now familiar coils of rope, barrels, and tubs of smelly fish. Men, both onboard ship and on the dock, talked loudly and shouted to one another as they worked at loading and unloading cargo.

Didda heard Einar shouted something. She turned slowly and walked backward a step, then stumbled. Swinging her arm out, she connected with soft hands steadying her.

"Oops, careful there!" A woman chuckled. "I've got her, Einar!" She shouted back toward the Gullfoss where the captain was standing at the rail. Didda lifted her hand in a wave to let him know she was all right.

"Well now, I guess introductions are in order." She smiled. "My name is Kristin Flosadottir and I'm from Einar's home town, Stykkisholmur. I'm a schoolteacher there."

"Nice meeting you, and thanks for catching me." Didda smiled as she politely stuck out her right hand.

Didda recognized the woman as the one she was on the ship last spring. Didda had thought she looked like a teacher and was pleased to find out she had been correct. Kristin grasped Didda's fingers with a very small hand that was surprisingly strong. She had a big smile on her friendly face, and her dark, hazel eyes were fringed with the longest eyelashes Didda had ever seen on any person. She was not pretty, but quite striking.

They walked about the village, as did most of the passengers. It felt good to walk on a surface that was not constantly moving under their feet. Some of them stopped for the ever-offered cup of coffee and sat down at tables that sat on solid ground.

When Didda saw couple of half-collapsed houses, she asked Kristin if she had heard about the previous year's earthquake in Dalvik.

"We didn't hear much back in our town, but captains and fishermen talk amongst themselves. I heard stories about how the quake caused gigantic waves to rise here in the fjord. A ship was tossed about in waves that men said were as high as those mountains."

Both of the gazed at the towering crags. Didda tried to imagine a wave of such monstrous proportion, but it was too mind-boggling. As they returned to the ship, Didda saw the two boys still fishing. She wondered where they had been last year when the quake happened and whether they had seen the humongous wave. She remembered how scared she and Lilla had been and they were far away when they felt the quake. It must have been so much scary to be right there when it happened.

"All aboard." The call came as the whistle blew.

The passengers on the dock scrambled up the gangplank and soon the ship was sailing out of the harbor and on its way to the next stop, Siglufjord. It was one of the northern-most fishing villages in Iceland. When they docked, both Kristin and Didda were astonish at the number of fishing boats crowded in the mountain-sheltered harbor. Many were flying flags from countries. As they strolled leisurely down the pier, they played a game to name the country for each flag. Didda could not identify many of them. As a teacher, Kristin knew many more but even she did not know them all.

The Gullfoss was still being unloaded when a great cry went up.

"The herring are running, the herring are running."

The effect was electric. Boats were scrambling to race out of the harbor, each one trying to out-maneuver the others. Everyone wanted to get into the open water as fast as possible and be the first to reach the enormous silver blanket of fish.

Far out in the mouth of the bay, those on shore saw the wide band of silvery sloshing of herring that seemed to stretch out to infinity. The heads of huge whales bobbed up, mouths wide open to gobble up millions of baby fish, while frantic seabirds screeched overhead and boats raced pell-mell into the melee.

The poor herring, Didda thought. Between men, whales and birds they did not have a chance.

A sudden squall of rain caused her and Kristin to run for the ship. Passengers that were walking on the pier were getting dripping wet from the unexpected shower. The rain pinged noisily against metal step, rail and smokestack of the ship. Then, just as quickly as it came, it left but the ocean and sky were turned an ugly, dark color.

The light was fading into gloomy grey by the time the crew had finished the loading and the ship was back on its journey. The grey-black mass of clouds was dropping toward the sea with amazing speed. Didda could no longer see the activity of the fishing boats that had set out earlier in so much excitement. Lights bobbing up and down among the deep, dark waves was the only indication of boats in the area.

Suddenly it seemed they were in a very different world. The weather became horrible. Rain started pelting down hard and at times almost sideways. They had sailed into the teeth of a gale coming from the direction of Greenland. The waves became huge. The hills of water towered higher and higher, and then rushed to meet them. The Gullfoss was lifted high into the air, then went down – down - down, then up - up - up again.

Didda wondered if the ship would just roll over and go down to the bottom of the sea like Ingi's boat. She felt a genuine stomach-gripping fear. What a horrible night to be out on the ocean.

Kristin had bid her goodnight earlier and gone below to her cabin. Didda was cowering under the steps that led to the pilothouse, out of the rain, but listened as the wind rose to an unnerving shriek. She covered her ears with both hands as she followed the seamen with terrified eyes. Water streamed from their rain-hats and ran into their faces, dripping into their beards. She watched as they steadied themselves, firmly gripping cables and rail. Some were even grinning as they went about their usual activities.

They are like Father, they love the sea even as awful as it can get. If they are not scared, I guess I do not have to be. But I am. I am really, really scared. Didda moved her hands from her ears to grab the underneath of the steps where she scrunched.

She thought about what happened to the 'unsinkable' Titanic, seamen still talked about how the ship collided with an ocean-floating iceberg.

Leaning forward she muttered, *I won't be afraid, I won't be afraid.*

Clamping her teeth, she peered around the steps to see if there were any icebergs near the ship. She nearly jumped a foot in the air when she felt a tap on her shoulder. She had not heard anyone coming. The noise from the howling wind and the smashing of the ocean against the ship drowned out everything else. The young man tapped her shoulder again and motioned up to the pilot's house where Einar was waving for me to come up.

Swaying and scrambling up the steps, both the young man and Didda were drenched by the time they reached the door. The wind almost tore the door out of Einar's hand as he reached for her. She was glad to be with him, but the view from here was even scarier than below. Einar tied her securely into a large chair to keep her safe. At times the ship was on top of waves that kind of eased out from under them, and then the ship would just drop and came down from the air with teeth-jarring thump. The Gullfoss wallowed, plunged and slopped seemingly in all directions, but actually was making a sluggish, steady gain toward Hornbjarg (Horn Cliff) peninsula.

As the saying goes in Iceland "Just wait a bit, this will change." By morning, the weather did change. Finally, feeling secure, Didda went to sleep in the pilothouse chair. She was still snoozing in the warm cabin when the weather broke. Einar woke her up to see icebergs glittering on the horizon. She watched a few straggling calves bouncing on the waves, heading to wherever the wind would take them.

The Captain skillfully steered the Gullfoss, skirting around the treacherous shore. Didda was glad the ship brought them safely through the long, wicked storm. The ship left the north fjords behind as they entered the west fjords

CHAPTER 23

The West Fjords

The northwest storm had pushed such massive ice from Greenland that all the fjords between Isafjord and Latrabjarg were packed with ice floes. Through a quirky pattern of wind and waves, their next stop was spared this colossal intrusion of icebergs.

There seemed to be an hundred boats that had taken shelter and anchored in the bay. In the harbor, two wooden piers ran out from the shore, the restless sea sending heavy waves sloshing up against the pilings. A black-and-red painted trawler and a small red fishing boat were moored at one pier, bouncing up and down with every billow. The Gullfoss eased up to the other dock.

Several people gathered to greet them with the news that some of the fjords where passengers were going to next were packed with ice. The Gullfoss would not be able to get through. The captain would decide if the Gullfoss would to stay here and hope the ice would break up soon, or go on to Stykkishólmur, which was the next and last stop before arriving in Reykjavik. The crew had been unloading the cargo meant for this village. Upon learning that some passengers were staying, the crew then unloaded both personal belongings and cargo originally intended for the ice-blocked villages.

Didda rubbed her chin as she observed the activities, squinting her right eye she intently watched the animated knot of people gathered at the end of the pier. Hands were wildly swinging and fingers were pointing to the mountain across the bay. Women appeared and grabbed children that were staring open-mouthed at the excited men. Voices were getting very loud and more men came running and yelling.

"We've got to get them. Now."

Already word was spreading like wildfire. Another polar bear had come ashore and the hunt was on. Didda was glad that the ship was now leaving she had no desire to see another pandemonium over a bear. They were on their way out of the fjord when a young passenger, who looked about eighteen, came by the rail where she and Kristin were, and stared intently toward the mountains on the eastern shore.

"I thought I saw a polar bear going up toward that glacier." He muttered as he removed his cap and scratched his head.

"Well, Bjarni. Why didn't you say something?" One of his friends exclaimed. "We could have had some real fun watching the locals go berserk!"

Watching for a while, as they sailed past the mountain range, they did not see any sign of a bear. Kristin went below deck to do some reading while Didda was back in her favorite spot, couching among the usual crates and ropes. A couple of old, yellow life-rings with faded letters that spelled Gullfoss on them were propped up by the crates. Didda stuck her feet into the hole of one of them, and as her eyes scoured the horizon, she was looking for icebergs and had every intention of shouting "Iceberg Ahead!" and thereby save the ship and all the passengers.

The ship turned south and they sailed past inky-black rock faces that rose steeply out of the sea. They were getting closer to Stykkishólmur. The ship was moving in much calmer waters and making good time. Passengers began to gather in little groups as the ship maneuvered up to the dock. Some were checking their bags; others were loudly discussing the bears.

"Man, that bear I saw loping up the country side towards the glacier was huge! I thought at first it was a white horse," said Bjarni. He scratched his left ear and adjusted his brown stocking cap pulling it down to his dark eyebrows.

"Maybe it was just a horse, Bjarni," one of his friends howled in merriment, slapping his thigh.

"But a horse doesn't lope - I saw a bear." His voice was now adamant.

The boys began to shout over the side of the ship to a group of young women who were calling and waving.

"You should have seen"

"Really humongous"

"Polar bears," Bjarni and his friends were whooping and shouting. The bear story was getting bigger and bigger.

Kristin and Didda grinned at each other. The story was getting outrageous by the time the gangplank was lowered and the guys ran down to the pier to meet the group of girls.

Kristin leaned over and whispered to Didda, "I can only imagine how many bears the story ends up having." Smiling at each other, they hugged one last time.

Kristin walked away with firm steps, down to the end of the pier, where she called out to a group of children who had been teasing seagulls. When they saw her, they started running and shouting, exuberantly throwing their arms around her. Two boys took Kristin's suitcases while other children hung unto her skirt. Didda sighed as they disappeared around a brown-rusted metal building.

Again, the Gullfoss sailed on.

Back Home in Reykjavik

The sun was dangling just at the horizon when they sailed between two flashing lighthouses and pulled into the harbor of Reykjavik.

Even though Didda had not wanted to leave Grandpa's farm, she was getting excited at the thought of seeing her mother and siblings. Her father was probably still out at sea so she did not expect to see him soon. She brushed back a strand of hair and waved at Einar who was very busy. She had already thanked him for his kindness and said her goodbyes. The crew seemed busier than ever since this was the last stop everyone will be getting leaving. Didda leaned at the rail with her two suitcases at her feet scanning the people huddled in groups on the pier.

She did not see her Mother but when she spotted her Father, she was the first one to jump on the plank when it was lowered. She flew toward the pier she flung herself into his arms. He tottered back and swung her around, chuckling, then put her down.

"You've grown a little taller, Diddamin, but still skinny as a rail." Grinning at her head to toe. "I trust you had a good trip. Einar told me you had a few encounters with icebergs and polar bears." He brushed hair from her face and kissed the tip of her nose.

This was quite unusual and Didda felt a little apprehension. "It's wonderful to see you, Father. I was expecting Mother to meet me, is she alright?" Didda tried to sound like this was nothing out of the ordinary. She turned as she heard a soft clearing of a throat behind her.

"Oh, thank you, Jon." Her father took her two suitcases out of the hands of the young seaman she had met on the ship. She had completely forgotten the bags in her excitement of seeing her father.

"The family is just fine." He assured her. "I'm meeting you because the Gullfoss arrived so early this morning, and my ship is docked just a couple of piers over."

He pointed where a black and orange painted trawler was anchored. Derricks and cranes cluttered the wharf to the delight of seagulls and other birds that perched up high, their screeching piercing the morning air. Ships and fishing boats were moored at various piers. Another fifty or so were anchored in the bay, their various national flags hanging limply in the wind-free air. A tugboat idly smoked near the entry of the harbor.

Turning back, Didda looked at the Gullfoss. She felt an odd urge to thank the stout ship for bringing them all safely home through those awful storms. That old tub did better than the fancy Titanic. She understood now why sailors and fishermen would get attached to a vessel that brought them home safely.

Didda's father started walking with the slow-rolling gait of a sailor she liked to imitate. She would take a long step, and then sway from side to side as if she were walking on a ship that was being pummeled on high seas. This often sent her two sisters into gales of laughter as they tried to imitate her. They usually ended in a squabble and Didda would get fighting mad, run into a room, and hide there with a book.

Today, as she walked with her father along the base of one pier the sea below them was gently moving. In the rare stillness, Didda heard ducks murmuring. Peeking over the edge, she saw them dipping their heads and paddling in formation under the wharf. An old skiff, broken and rotted out, lay on the rocks of the shore, a perfect perch for the hoard of seabird fluttering around.

As they reached the second pier, they turned to go towards the ship. A boy, who looked about Didda's age, was sitting with his bare feet hanging over the edge of the dock, the legs of his trousers rolled up and over his bony knees. A fishing line without a bait on its hook dangled from his hands. Three fish, a good two-feet-long each, wriggled in a hemp-bag lying by his side. His wrinkled red shirt was partly tucked into the waist of his pants. He had pulled his black wool cap down to his almost-white eyebrows, and completely covered his hair.

"Good morning. Fish looks good." Didda's father remarked as he touched the bag with his right toe. The boy turned, nodded and motioned for them to look down into the water. Didda could not believe her eyes. The fish were in thick layers, flopping and sloshing over each other in the sea. The boy had just dropped his fish line into the chaotic mess and pulled up his catch without a bait!

Looking up the boy grinned, his green-blue eyes gleeful. "You know the saying, 'fish is food on the table and gold in the pocket' Cap'n,"

"How right you are, son. How right you are." Her father tipped his right hand to his cap as she waved at the boy. A shout from the trawler got their attention.

"Hallo, Captain, breakfast is ready."

"That's our cook, Juan. Are you hungry?" Her father asked just as her stomach growled loudly and she nodded.

An odd-looking man was leaning over the rail. He looked just like the way Didda imagined a pirate would look. His black Kung-Fu mustache draped over the lower half of his swarthy face. Dark eyebrows went from the left of his brow, dipped over his nose, then continued to the right of his forehead in one full line. He made Didda think of a dark raven in flight. His dark eyes were piercing and he scared the daylights out of her. But, boy, could he cook.

They boarded the ship and made their way to the crew dining area. The table was loaded with cheese, boiled eggs, fish balls, dark bread and hot, strong, coffee. Didda's fears melted away like ice cubes in a fiery lava flow.

CHAPTER 25

Mother Falls into Volcanic Crevasse

Didda, her sisters, and her brothers were at the summer home enjoying their last vacation before school started. They were fishing, splashing in the ice-cold creek, and, when the wind died down enough for the water to be still, skipping stones across the surface. They had quite a competition to see how many times each rock would skip before sinking.

Other times they would find small lava rocks that would float. This fascinated Didda's youngest brother, Frankie, the most. He would look under the pumice to see what made it move.

"There should be a motor," He would fuss. His brothers and sisters showed him how to throw pebbles to cause waves in the water so he could see his little 'boat' wobble and bobble. Didda picked up a stick and stirred the water to create a little more movement

"See, that's how the Vikings looked at the current," Didda said. "They didn't have a motor on their long-boats, only oars. They studied the waves to see which way to go for their discoveries."

Frankie was satisfied with that answer. He like to hear stories about the Vikings, as they all did. Frankie could lay on his stomach for hours watching his 'Viking boat' move.

The widest part of the creek that ran across the field in front of the little house was pond-like, and shone like a mirror on this particular afternoon. The fish plopped up and down, pink and silver scales shining in the elusive sun. Wispy, raggedy clouds hung in the grey-blue sky.

A group of seagulls hopped on the rail of the wood bridge that spanned the creek. Cocking and puffing up their wings, they watched the fish jump in and out of the water. This was their last day here and it was unusually still and mild. The mountain range was hidden by soft, lazily floating, grey-white fog. Iceland's most wicked volcano,

Hekla, sat quietly in the distance, her perpetual white fluff hanging over her in the sky. The only other house, barely in sight, was a farm across the creek. They called them the 'rich people' because their farm was so large.

The farmer there raised pigs, which was not very well thought of by the sheep farmers. Didda and Lilla were sitting on the top step outside their cabin. They were finishing a long necklace that they were making from the dandelions they had picked and snipped off the blooms. They had made a bracelet and a necklace that now decorated Lilla. Now they were working on a necklace for Sissi.

"Do you have the scissors?" Lilla asked, running her hand under the dandelion's waste.

"No I don't have them. Maybe you are sitting on them, or maybe the Hidden Folk needed to borrow them." Didda searched half-heartedly around her. "If they borrowed them, you know the scissors will turn up, The Folks always return stuff."

Scowling, Lilla stood up.

A horrendous scream tore through the air and crying echoed around them. As they jumped up and ran down the steps, they saw Sissi tearing across the lava field. She had her skirt hiked up high with both hands so she could run faster. She stumbled and cried when the Didda and Lilla reached her. She sputtered and cried so much neither one could understand her words. A short distance away, Didda saw Frankie sitting on the ground, mouth wide open crying "mamma, mamma." Buddy was on his stomach, arms flailing and feet kicking in the air. He was looking into what seemed to be a narrow split in the moss-covered ground.

"What happened to Mamma?" Lilla cried.

"She fell - crack in the ground. I thought I heard ..her.. heard cry out, but she's awful quiet," Sissi fought to speak the words and swallowed hard, tears running down her cheeks. "We have to get help!"

"We'll have to get help from the pig-farmer." Didda turned to Sissi, who was wiping her face with her skirt.

"I'll get him, Sissi. You're the oldest so you have to stay with Mamma and the little ones." Didda started running for the creek.

"Don't you dare," both of her sisters screamed in unison.

Didda stopped, and stared at them. "What else can we do? They are the only people close by. We've got to get help."

Her stomach was in knots, she had no idea how badly her mother might be hurt, but she knew she could not waste time. The lava rocks could be razor sharp and cuts could be very deep. Sissi had indicated that their mother might be unconscious.

"You're gonna get killed." Lilla shrieked. "Remember what happened the last time!"

Ignoring their protests, Didda turned and started running toward the distant farm. Getting to the creek, she wadded up her skirt into a knot and stomped into the ice-cold rushing water that came up to her knees. She saw the young roan just on the other side.

Didda remembered quite clearly, what happened the last time. She had disobeyed and gone across this same creek and jumped on this same colt, which promptly bucked her off and knocked her out cold. She had promised, 'cross my heart' never to go over that creek again. But this is an emergency.

Carefully, Didda crawled up the bank on the other side. This time she was not going to surprise the horse. She talked to him with chattering teeth. Then, taking a running leap, she jumped on his back. Snorting fiercely and shaking his head, he took off as if he had been whacked on the rump. This time, she was ready. She fastened her legs tightly to his smooth back and clenched both of her fists into his tossing mane as he galloped toward the farmhouse.

As she neared the huge pigpen, the farmer came running toward her, purple-faced, both fists angrily pounding the air. Then leaping, he grabbed his horse by the neck and quickly brought him to a halt, as he growled at Didda.

"I told you the last time if you ever," He stopped as he saw her terrified, red-blotched face.

"All right, girl. Do not look so scared. I'm not going to hurt you, but you really," He broke off and scowled.

"It's Ma…ma" Didda stammered as she slid off the horse, and explained what had happened.

She was surprised how gentle this horrible, bad-tempered pig farmer became. Patting her on the head, he turned, and whistled for his older horse. The horse promptly came running.

The farmer roared, "Helga come here."

"Coming, Arni," a woman turned from the clothesline where she'd been pinning snow-white sheet. The snapping sound of wet clothes followed her as she slowly plodded closer to her husband. Then she stopped. Furious, she knit her black heavy brows, and fastened her gimlet eyes on Didda. Helga was large of bone and feature, and looked very strong. Didda was scared to death of her, too, even when she did not look so grim.

Firmly she placed her hand on her ample hips and glared. "You are really in trouble now. I've got a good mind to."

"Hold on, Helga." Arni held up his right palm. "We have an emergency. Her mother is hurt. Grab your first-aid kit and come on over. I will go now and take the child with me. I am amazed she was able to hold on to this un-broken colt." Arni was putting the reins on his horse as he spoke. Swinging his right foot over the horse' back, he moved and made room for Didda in front of him. Then, he reached down as she lifted up her hands.

Arni gave his horse a smart whack and they went on a brisk gallop across the lava-field. They sloshed across the creek where Lilla and Buddy were waiting, faces wet and streaky with tears. They rode on to where Sissi was waiting. She was holding Frank, rocking back and crooning. They both looked up as Didda and Arni rode up. Arni dismounted and lifted Didda off the horse. She ran to Sissi and all the children were trying to talk at the same time.

"Mother is all right. She can talk but she hurts." They babbled as Arni knelt down and looked into the crevasse.

"Hallo, Dagbjort. Talk to me," he said. "How are you hurt? Can you move at all?"

"I'm glad you're here Arni" She gasped. "I'm alright but I can't move my right ankle without hurting pretty bad."

"Helga is riding up now. She will come down and look at your foot. We'll get you out of there pretty soon," Arni assured her.

Helga came riding up at a flying pace. She had tied her skirt up between her legs so she appeared to be wearing black, billowy bloomers, making for easier bareback riding. Didda was impressed with the interesting design. In one surprisingly fluid motion, Helga was off the horse and kneeling down by her husband.

Lilla and Didda had climbed on top of a boulder so they would be out of the way. Buddy and Frankie sat on the moss below their feet, while Sissi stood beside Arni, ready to help.

Helga carefully scrambled down into the hole. Didda could hear the murmur of the two

"No broken bones, Arni." Helga called to her husband. "I will wrap her ankle so we can move her. First, hand me your bottle. We had better give her a stiff drink." As he handed her the bottle they could hear the two women giggling like couple of schoolgirls. Helga's hand came up and something seemed to be wadded up in it.

"Look here, Arni, our little Kisa was down here. I didn't know she'd wandered off." She lifted a small, coal-black mewling fur ball to her husband. Arni gently stroked the small head with his big hands then handed the bundle to Frankie, who was in awe of the purring creature.

After careful lifting and pulling, the couple were able to get Dag-bjort out of the crevasse. The fissure was only six feet deep but had sharp, jagged cinder rocks on the bottom. She had landed on the side of her right foot, hitting her head on the edge of the rift as she fell in. She had a large bump on the back of her head. Helga had wrapped her right foot from toe to knee. Didda could not imagine how anyone could jam so much bandage into such a small emergency kit.

"I feel like such silly sheep, falling in like that. I thought I heard a child cry, but it was the kitten. I could feel the brittle shale giving away at the edge, but I couldn't stop myself from falling." She shook her head then groaned and grabbed her head in her hands, then, looking up she saw Lilla and Didda sitting on top of the rock.

"Sissi, get the girls off of there. They know better." She murmured.

Didda looked at Lilla as they scurried down. Yes indeed, they knew better. Mother had told them numerous times not to climb on that particular rock. Remember your cousin who limps? She got that way because she climbed a huge rock that was known to be the Hidden's Castle. They do not take kindly to kids that climb on top of their buildings. She had warned them.

Fearful, Didda looked behind her as she and Lilla followed Sissi, who had Frankie and Buddy by a hand. Frankie had the kitten wrapped up in his sweater, protecting the bundle with his free hand. She did not see any angry beings, but she walked a little faster, dragging Lilla with her.

Arni and Helga crossed their hands together and formed a seat for Dagbjort to sit. She wrapped an arm over the neck of each of them and they all walked slowly toward the cabin to wait for Elsa. The farm couple offered to stay with them but Dagbjort assured them that the nanny would be on the evening bus. They had planned for her help to close up the cabin for the winter. She thanked them for their kindness then Didda and the other children stepped outside to wave as they rode off. They had been so kind, even after Didda had caused them trouble. She hoped that she would never again judge a person based on other people's opinions.

Sissi herded them all back inside and got them started on packing. Later, Buddy, Lilla and Didda stood by the side of the road and watched the rattling bus lumber up the volcanic-cinder, one-lane road. Elsa stepped down and immediately they started talking at the same time

"Mother fell into a crevasse," Didda started.

"She hurt her head and foot," Lilla hopped around Elsa.

"The pig-farmer and his wife came," Buddy said, excitedly.

"Whoa, hold it. One at a time." Elsa stopped. "Your Mother is all right?"

They all nodded vigorously. The details of the story poured out, from the terrifying fall to the miraculous rescue and the children led Elsa to the cabin.

The next morning, the weather had changed. A hard northeast gale was blowing across the lava field. Dark-grey clouds scudded across the somber sky. The whole family and Nanny Elsa bundled up in heavy sweaters and knit caps as they sat by the road. Their suitcases were at their feet. Didda heard the rattling old bus drive up and saw it swing into their lane and stop. Elsa spoke with Skuli, the bus driver, for a minute. Then both of them walked up to the cabin and went inside. Soon they came back out carrying a bundled-up Mother the same way as Arni and Helga had done.

Walking down the lane and over the wood bridge was a good distance and both Elsa and Skuli were breathing hard as they reached the bus. By the time Dagbjort was settled and pillows were cushioned under her foot she looked very pale.

It was even more depressing than the end of summer usually was. In just three days and she would be back in school. Didda dreaded it.

CHAPTER 26

Ollie the Bully

Goa and Didda stomped grumpily down the crowded blue-painted hallway that smelled strongly of green lye-soap. Neither of them were happy to be back in school. They were both teased unmercifully, Didda, because of her name, and Goa, because she stuttered.

They entered the classroom where Ollie, the biggest bully, was sitting with two of his friends. Didda's heart sank. She was destined to put up with those hooligans forever. To make matters worse, her desk was in front of Ollie's, giving him perfect opportunity to annoy her. Didda just knew he would yank on her hair and whisper taunts without detection from the teacher. Gnawing her lower lip, Didda could feel her face grow red-hot as her temper rose ten-degrees.

"Good morning, children. My name is Inga, and I'll be your teacher this year."

She was disgustingly cheerful as she swung a blue and white-checkered towel over her shoulder. On her left arm hung a small tin bucket, and in the other hand she had a bottle full of shimmering, sickly-yellow oily liquid. She had a large tablespoon in her right hand that she jabbed in the air as she spoke.

"You know the routine of first things first." She chuckled as if she were enjoying a huge joke.

Didda brushed strands of hair from her face and looked at Goa, who was sitting in front of her. She could see the red flush creep across the back of Goa's neck, blending with her red hair. Slowly she turned, they rolled their eyes at each other - the cod-liver oil. Didda's mouth went dry. She desperately tried to think of some way to get out of having to take the oil.

Feet heavy, they obediently shuffled to the front of the room, where Miss Inga waited.

"Hold your nose and open wide, Goa." Inga's voice was positively chirping.

Didda wondered how the teacher could be so chipper. She had to know how much all the students hated that stuff. Didda knew she was going to throw up, right there in front of everyone. Ollie and his friends would never let up on the teasing and name-calling. She would never be able to come back, or maybe she would get lucky, choke on the stuff and just die on the spot. Didda grit her teeth. If she kept gritting her teeth like that, it would be her luck to be just like toothless old Olga. Unconsciously, she snapped her fingers just as she had been practicing for so long.

Suddenly she relaxed. She bit the inside of her lip to keep from giggling. She had forgotten Sigga's advice about handling bullies. She sat up straight in her seat as Inga stood by her desk and happily sang out.

"Hold your nose and open wide, Didda." Didda heard Ollie snicker behind her and whisper.

She turned and hissed, "I gave your name-calling to the trolls." She smiled sweetly at the teacher, who was looking at Ollie. Inga's smile was replaced by a tight frown knit between her green eyes.

Pinching her nose with her thumb and fingers of her right hand, Didda opened her mouth wide for Inga to pour in a spoonful of the stomach-churning stuff. With heroic effort, she managed to swallow nonchalantly. The teacher nodded her a couple of times then turned to Ollie.

"Your turn, Ollie. Hold your nose"

"That's girl stuff. I don't need to hold my nose," he boasted. The spoon clicked against his teeth as Inga poured the gooey yellow oil into his mouth.

"Swallow." Teacher's voice was frim, no longer cheerful.

Didda heard Ollie's strangled gulp and turned just in time to see him turn grey-green, gag violently, and then throw up into the bucket Inga was holding. With a wicked smirk on her face, Didda leered into his face of her tormentor and snapped her fingers. Her antagonist's eyes glared at her.

They had three weeks of unusually warm autumn days where they had been able to enjoy the out-of-doors before weather took a nasty turn. Rain turned to sleet and Mount Esja, across from Reykjavik, was covered in white from her top to the seashore. Rime covered the walkway to the school, and icicles hung from the metal pipes that formed the handrails.

Didda got her regrettable, second revenge.

Sissi, Lilla, Goa and Didda arrived at school, all bundled up. They carefully walked up the icy steps as Ollie and two of his friends watched, gleefully waiting for a fall or other misfortune. A metal flagpole was fastened at a slant to the iron rail. The Icelandic flag hung limply in the sleet. Ollie had perched himself up on the rail and grabbed the flagpole with his bare left hand.

"Didda…GoGoGo…." The boys started their taunting.

"Ollie - Get your hand off of that pole." Miss Inga's voice was shrill with alarm. She had just stepped out to ring the school bell and saw his unprotected hand.

Startled, Ollie slid down and slipped, still holding on to the pole. Her warning came too late. His hand was stuck. His face swung against the pole and he opened his mouth to yell, but all he could do was grunt. His eyes bulged in terror. The tip of his tongue was frozen to the iron flagpole.

Teachers came running out when the girls started screaming. Miss Inga leaned down and held Ollie's head to keep him from moving. One group of teachers shoo'd children inside to their classrooms. Others grouped around Miss Inga and Ollie to assess the situation. One was sent to the cafeteria for boiling water. The hot water was quickly brought out and poured on the pole. In a short time, Ollie was free but a little worse for the wear. His left palm was sore for a few days and it was a while before he was able to speak properly.

Didda behaved, she did not sneer at all and did not make fun of him. She actually felt sorry for him. She did not really think the trölls had anything to do with his accident, but she was not certain. To be safe, the decided it was best not to snap her fingers and give her problems to them. She was better off solving problems herself.

Anyway, Christmas is coming and she knew she had better be good. If not, Yule lads will put a rotten potato in her shoe instead of leaving something nice. And the Yule Lads were not trölls to be messed with.

CHAPTER 27

Christmas

Didda was excited for Christmas every year, but this year was extra special. Her family did not celebrate many holidays, just the major ones. Every year, they would have a special celebration only for Christmas, New Year Eve, Easter, Bolludaginn (Bun Day), Ash Wednesday, and Easter. They never celebrated the minor things like birthdays and those days would pass unnoticed with no parties or gifts.

What made the Christmas of 1935 was even more special was the fact that Father was home. He had arrived back home after a fishing trip to England and was quieter than usual. Didda heard him speaking a few time with Mother in a hushed voice about a war in Europe. Didda did not pay much attention. She thought that Europe was far away and a war there would not affect their small isolated island.

She had no time to think of such scary or depressing things. Father was taking them to a Seamen's Christmas Party held at the Opera House. They rushed around to get ready in their best clothes.

It was cold and the water line had frozen. Hanna brought in a dish-pan full of snow and melted it for the children to bathe. Hanna helped the boys get dressed, while Dagbjort supervised her daughters. She brushed their hair and helped them carefully arrange the locks. The girls dressed under their Mother's supervision. It was a special oc-casion and required the traditional Icelandic dress. Each of the girls wore a black skirt and a white blouse, topped with a red vest ornately embroidered with gold thread. Each had a tasseled cap on her head. The boys wore green jackets with their short breeches tucked into their long socks just below the knees. Once they were ready, Dagbjort lined them up and had them turn a few time to make sure the small group was presentable.

Didda felt like an overstuffed sausage once she was bundled up against the winter blast. Her brothers and sisters lined up next to her did not fare much better. She watched as beads of sweat gathered on Lilla's upper lip. Thankfully, their wait was short and they quickly waddled downstairs. Didda felt like this was a magical night. Father had extravagantly called for a taxi. It was decrepit and old, but still seemed like a luxury.

All the church bells in the capital of Reykjavik were chiming at the same time, ushering the start of the Christmas Season. The Icelandic holiday started promptly at 6:00 p.m. on the 24th of December. The loud ringing of the bells added to the festive air.

The dark-blue sky was lit up with pinkish-green, shimmering curtains of rapidly moving lights. The Aurora Borealis, Northern Lights, were in full display. The ribbons of red, gold, and purple streaks shot across the sky in a breathtaking show. Up and down, side-to-side the lights danced across the heavens. Didda craned her neck this way and that, pointing to Sissi, *ooh-ing* and *ahh-ing* over each wonder. Frankie and Buddy pushed and climbed over each other and Lilla, jostling for a better view.

With much excitement, they kids erupted out of the cab and into the entry of the Opera House. Didda saw her father stop to greet someone as her mother grasped her arm.

"Stay together, Diddamin, it's too cold outside," Dagbjort said as she ushered the group of children inside.

Suddenly, Lilla stopped short and Didda ran into her.

"Hey," she complained but then her voice trailed off.

The giant Christmas tree at the party was awesome, its top reached clear up to the vaulted ceiling. The few trees that grew in Iceland never reached such massive height. Didda knew it had to come here on one of the ships from some far-off country.

She threw her head back and craned to see the top. The hundreds of lighted candles flickered in the huge ballroom. Red, green, yellow, and white paper-chains were wrapped around and around, from top to bottom. Various sized and intricately shaped bags were hanging from the branches, each bag bulging to overflowing with hard candy.

Music filled the room. The rollicking accordion and violin blended together with a holiday tune that reverberated through the air. Children darted around, family stood in small knots, talking with friends and neighbors. Didda stood, mesmerized, rooted to the wood floor. She could feel the ground under her feet shaking and crackling like aftershocks of an earthquake. Children in formed a circle and were hopping, clomping, and swinging in a dance around the tree. As twirled by, hands reached out and grabbed Sissi, Lilla and Didda, pulling them into the dance. Buddy joined in, grabbing the hand of the next dancer.

Frankie could not stop staring at the tree. He stumbled and tottered around, blue eyes scrunched half-shut, as he followed his mother.

"What's the matter with your eyes? Why are you closing them like that?" Dagbjort was concerned.

Frankie was like one hypnotized.

"When I squeeze my eyes it makes hundreds and hundreds of lights, maybe millions, maybe a gazillion trillion lights!" Frankie whispered in awe.

Frankie did not quit squinting until the candy bags and oranges were handed out. They were a happy but tired bunch that went home that night, chattering in excitement what tomorrow was going to bring.

Didda woke up Christmas morning and breathed in deeply. The aroma of cardamom, cinnamon, and vanilla coming from the kitchen surrounded her. Gróa was baking kleinur, a traditional Icelandic twist-cookie, and Pönnukökur, a very thin crepe-like pancake. The Pönnukökur were spread with jam, folded up, and then topped them with dollop of whipped cream. Mother folded the pancake in half and again in half, so it looked like a triangle. They needed forks to eat the rich, yummy treat.

"Lilla! Sissi!" Didda shouted, "Get up – it's Christmas" shaking her sisters excitedly as she climbed over them. They scrambled to dress and hurried downstairs.

"Well, the sleepyheads decided to join us," Dagbjort said, grinning.

Gróa was already helping Frankie and Buddy fill their plates. Didda, Sissi, and Lilla slid into the empty seats and dug in.

After the family had eaten and Hanna had cleared the table, Didda's father told them all to sit down in the living room and wait. He quickly disappeared into the bedroom.

Didda's toes tingled in anticipation. They never had store-bought toys, always got something carved or knitted. Each item was hand-made with the recipient in mind and sometimes they each received an orange with their gift. They would put the orange-peel in a glass of water with a spoonful of sugar and let it sit overnight. It made a wonderful orange juice the next morning.

Father came out with his arms loaded with boxes, full of stuff from his trip to England. He handed a tuck to Buddy as the other children clamored around him. Buddy, for a change, was speechless for a moment, and then he whooped and fell to the floor with the truck. Frankie received a truck as well. He inspected it from end to end, looked under it, and turned to his mother, his eyes sparkling.

"This is the biggest and the best." He breathed.

Each of the girls received an almost life-size plastic baby-doll. Didda was overjoyed. This Christmas was beyond her wildest dreams!

A few days after Christmas, Didda could not find her baby-doll. She searched her room and the living room, and then walked to the kitchen to check for her baby there. As she drew closer, she heard a voice muttering. Entering the kitchen, Didda found Buddy there alone, still muttering. She fought back a giggle. A devious thought popped into her head and without a second's hesitation, she crept up, intending to jump and scream to scare him.

"Are you scared yet?" Buddy whispered.

Didda wondered what game he was playing. She slipped through the doorway and tiptoed up behind him. She gasped. He held a lighted candle in his hand, waving it close to the nose of her doll. Didda's eyes widened, unable to believe what she was witnessing.

"Are you scared yet?" He bent closer as Didda opened her mouth to scream.

Suddenly, there was a sound of a hissing sizzle, then *pouf!* The plastic baby-doll disappeared in a flash.

Shocked, Didda stood with her mouth still open. No sound came out. She stared at the tiny, weird-shaped, pink blob that had been her beloved Christmas present. She looked up and into the bulging eyes and white face of Buddy, who slowly sank to his knees, and then lay flat on the floor, unconscious.

Didda started screaming. She knew her doll was dead and was certain her brother was too. A couple of days later, both Buddy and Didda were fine. Another adventure was already scheduled and their minds were now on the New Year's Eve festivities and New Year's Day Dinner.

It was twilight-dark although it was only four in the afternoon. A group of seven, two adults and five children stepped outside to catch the downtown bus. Didda, Sissi and Lilla skipped ahead. Dagbjort and Gróa followed and kept a close watch on Buddy and Frankie. They were all looking forward to the exciting New Year's Eve event. Small bonfires burned at various places in Reykjavik, but the biggest one was downtown in a cleared field. As they neared the celebration, the bonfire was being prepared The pile of wood from old boats, tires, and anything burnable seemed as tall as a house.

The small group found a spot that offered a good view and they sat on the ground to wait for the show to begin. Didda looked up into the dark-blue sky where she saw what she thought to be a gazillion-trillion stars twinkling. In a microseconds there was a huge multicol-ored, spiral-curtain sparkling and moving fast. Suddenly, purple and green streaked patches broke away from the curtain and leaped across the entire sky in an awesome show for several minutes. The colors floated off and away, only to come back and move side to side in amazing display of bright colors that looked like fractured rainbows. The Northern Lights were beautiful.

As the bonfire was lit and the huge pile was burning to the sky, people started dancing around in a huge circle, welcoming the New Year. Brennivín and coffee flowed generously.

People began belting out folk songs and singing at the top of their voices. Didda enjoyed the great spectacle, but she thought that the Au-rora Borealis was far more impressive and memorable. It was a quite frequent and welcome show during the long dark Icelandic winters, but she never tired of watching it.

Didda and her family always went to Aunt Þrúður and Uncle Jón's house for dinner on New Year Day. Aunt Þrúður was her mother's sister, and Didda thought she was rich. They lived in a beautifully furnished place above their store and they had a piano. Didda did not know of anyone else with a piano in their home. The steps in the foyer, leading to the upstairs, had a brass edges polished to a mirror-like finish each. Didda would tiptoe and admire each elegant step all the way up to the top.

Jón always sat at the head of the table and Aunt Þrúður at the other end. After a scrumptious dinner of smoked mutton, creamed potatoes, boiled eggs, and other goodies, plus cream-torte for dessert, each of the children would approach the hosts for a formal thank you, first to Aunt and then to Jón. In proper form, Didda extended her right hand, put her right toe behind her left heel, bend her knees while holding unto the hem of her dresses with her left hand, and give a nice curtsy. Her sisters did the same, while Buddy and Frankie bent deep from their waist and bowed quite elegantly.

Buddy *never* acted up at Aunt Þrúður's home.

CHAPTER 28

Jólasveinarnir The Yule Lads

In preparation for Christmas, Didda and her brothers and sisters, like most of the children in Iceland, had completed the annual traditional ritual. On December twelfth, they each placed a pair of shoes on the windowsill. Every day, they were careful to be on their best behavior. Didda was super-careful because of the Yule Lads.

Her mother had told her many stories about Grýla, the horrible tröll, her tröll-ogre husband, Leppaludi, and their terrible tröll family. The trölls would chase and grab a hold of naughty kids.

The tröll couple had hundreds of tröll children, and all would delight in causing mischief among folks. Didda heard many of the stories from Uncle Bibbi. His story about the Yule Lads was the one that caused their concern during Christmas-time. Grýla has thirteen tröll sons that were on the lookout at Christmas for children who misbehaved. She sent her sons out to snatch ng naughty children and stick them into huge black burlap-bags they slung over their grotesquely lumpy shoulders. They would then take the naughty kids to their Monster-Mamma. Once Grýla had the children, she would lock them up in a mountain cave and eventually eat them.

Didda had never heard of any kids caught by the Yule Lads. She thought maybe there were not that many truly bad kids, or maybe only the truly bad ones could out-run the trölls. If the trölls even did sneak down from the mountain and steal kids. She was not sure what to believe.

Uncle Bibbi said that the stories of the Yule Lads mellowed and most people did not believe that the trölls would steal bad children. Bibbi said that over hundreds of years, the trölls became nicer and somewhere along the way, they started leaving small presents in the shoes of the good kids. However, a piece of black lava-rock, or worse yet, a rotten potato, would be in the shoes of the naughty children.

Just the thought of getting a rotten potato in her shoe made Didda try very hard to be good. She, like every child in Iceland knew the names of the Jólasveinar, and read about them in the poem by Jóhannes from Kötlum. Uncle Bibbi read it to Didda, with Sissi, Lilla, Frankie and Buddy gathered around. He would whisper and read to them from one of his books:

> Let me tell the story
> of the lads of few charms,
> who once upon a time
> used to visit our farms.
>
> Thirteen altogether,
> these gents in their prime
> didn't want to irk people
> all at one time.
>
> They came from the mountains,
> as many of you know,
> in a long single file
> to the farmsteads below.
>
> Creeping up, all stealth,
> they unlocked the door.
> The kitchen and the pantry
> they came looking for.

Stekkastaur---Sheep-Cote Clod, the first Yule Lad comes to town December the 12th

> He came stiff as wood,
> to prey upon the farmer's sheep
> as far as he could.
> He wished to milk the ewes,
> but it was no accident

he couldn't; he had stiff knees
-not to convenient.

***

Giljagaur -- December 13th came **Gully Gawk** (or Crevasse Imp) this
lad likes to hide in gullies and wait for opportunity to steal milk.

The second was Gully Gawk;
grey his head and mien,
He snuck into the cow-barn
from his craggy ravine
Hiding in the stalls,
he would steal the milk, while
the milkmaid gave the cowherd
a meaningful smile.

***

Stúfur ---Shorty, or Stubby, the shortest of the brothers, arrived in the
14th.

Stubby was the third called,
a stunted little man,
who watched for every chance
to whisk off a pan.
And scurrying away with it,
he scraped off the bits
that stuck to the bottom
and brims - his favorites.

***

Skeiðisleikir--- Spoon-Licker came down from the mountains on 15th of December.

> The fourth was Spoon Licker,
> like spindle he was thin.
> He felt himself in clover
> when the cook wasn't in.
> Then stepping up, he grappled
> the stirring spoon with glee,
> holding it with both hands
> for it was slippery.

***

Pottaskefilll---Pot-scraper (or Pot-Licker) is expected on December the 16th.

> Pot Scraper, the fifth one,
> was a funny sort of chap.
> When kids were given scrapings,
> he'd come to the door and tap.
> And they would rush to see
> if there really was a guest.
> Then he hurried to the pot
> and had a scraping fest.

***

Áskasleikir---Bowl Licker, came to town on December the 17th.

> Bowl licker, the sixth one,
> was shockingly ill bred.

From underneath the bedsteads
he stuck his ugly head.
And when the bowls were left
to be licked by dog or cat
he snatched them for himself
- he was sure good at that!

***

Hurðaskellir---Door-slammer, came to town on December the 18th.

The seventh was Door Slammer,
a sorry, vulgar chap:
When people in the twilight
would take a little nap,
he was happy as a lark
with the havoc he would wreak,
slamming doors and hearing
the hinges on the squeak.

***

Skygámur---Yogurt Gobbler---On the 19th Yogurt Gobbler makes his appearance.

Yogurt Gobbler was the eight,
was an awful stupid bloke.
He lambasted the yogurt tub
till the lid on it broke
Then he stood there, gobbling
-his greed was well known-

until, about to burst,
he would bleat, howl and groan.

***

Bjúgnakrækir---Sausage-Swiper---shows up on December the 20th.

The ninth was Sausage Swiper,
a shifty pilferer.
He climbed up to the rafters
and raided food from there
Sitting on a crossbeam
In soot and in smoke,
he fed himself on sausage
fit for gentlefolk.

***

Gluggagægir---Window Peeper---This one starts his peeping on the 21st.

The tenth was Window Peeper,
a weird little twit,
who stepped up to the window
and stole a peek through it.
And whatever was inside
to which his eye was drawn,
he most likely attempted
to take later on.

***

Gáttaþefur---Door Sniffer, he comes around December 22nd.

> Eleventh was Door Sniffer,
> A doltish lad and gross.
> He never got a cold, yet had
> A huge sensitive nose.
> He caught the scent of lace bread
> While league away still
> And ran toward it weightless
> As wind over dale and hill.

***

Ketkrógur---Meat Hook---arrives on December 23rd. St. Thórlák's Day.

> Meat Hook, the twelfth one,
> his talent would display
> as soon as he arrived
> on Saint Thórláks Day.
> He snagged himself a morsel
> of meat of any sort,
> although his hook at times was
> a tiny bit short.

***

Kertasníkir---Candle Beggar---came on December 24th. He longed to have his very own candle.

> The thirteenth was Candle Beggar
> -'twas cold, I believe,

if he was not the last
of the lot on Christmas Eve.
He trailed after the little ones
who, like happy sprites,
ran about the farm with
their fine tallow lights.

This popular poem about the Yule Lads was written by the late Jóhannes from Kötlum, and first appeared in the book "Jólin Koma" (Christmas is coming) in 1932.

GLOSSARY

A, Á

Akureyri; Second largest town in Iceland, situated in the north.

B

Breiðifjörður; Wide fjord (bay), west Iceland

D, Ð (say soft 'th')

Djúpivogur; Deep Cove

E É

Eldfell; Fire Mountain

Eyjafjallajökull; Island Mountain Glacier.

Eyjafjörður; Island Fjord

F

Flatey; Flat Island

Færeyjar; islands situated in the Atlantic Ocean between Iceland and Norway.

G

Gullfoss; Golden Falls

Goðafoss; The Falls of The Gods.

H

Heimaey; Iceland's largest island

Helgafell; Holy Mountain

Höfn; Harbor

I Í

Ísafjörður; Fjord of Ice

J

Jökullsár; Glacier River

Jökullsárlón; Glacier River Bay.

K

Kría; Arctic tern.

L

Lagarfljót; Lake Handsome.

Lagarfljótsormurin; The Worm of Lake Handsome.

Lögberg; Law Rock (situated at Þingvellir)

Lækjartorg; Downtown square Reykjavik

M

Mývatn; Midge Lake (no mosquito in all of Iceland!)

Mýrdalsjökull; Glacier jof Mýrdal

P

Papey; Pope (or Monk) Island

R

Reykjavik; Capital of Iceland

Reyðarfjörður; Red (?) Fjord

S

Snæfellsjökull; Snow Mountain Glacier

Smörfjell; Butter Mountain

Siglufjörður; Fjord of Sails.

Skjálfandi: Trembling (shivering) Bay

V

Vatn; Water.

Vatnajökull; Glacier of Water.

Vestmanneyjar; West Men Island

Vopnafjörður; Fjord of Weapons

Þ (say hard <u>th</u>)

Þing; Parliament

Þingvellir; Old time meeting place of Parliament, congress.

Æ (say "I")

Æðarfugl; Eider bird (Eider duck).

Ö

Öræfarjökull

ICELANDIC LANGUAGE

Explanation of selected word endings

----fell mountain (s)

----fjall

----fjörður fjord

----vogur

----vík bay,cove

----flói

----ey island

----eyja

---- jökull glacier

EXAMPLE Eyjafjallajökull: Eyja - fjalla - jökull --- Island mountain glacier.

Pronunciation

Áá,say like in ouch - how

Ðð‹›this - the

Éé‹›yet - yell

Íí‹›eek - eel

Óó‹›over - no

Úú‹›l<u>oo</u>t - m<u>oo</u>t

Þþ‹›<u>th</u>ing - <u>th</u>orn

Ææ‹›I - <u>I</u>ce

Öö‹›h<u>u</u>rry - h<u>u</u>rt

The letter "C" is not used in any Icelandic words.

About the Author

Íeda Jónasdóttir grew up in Iceland, a country often called *The Land of Fire And Ice.*

In 1944, at age nineteen she attended a USO dance and met an American service man, Del Herman, stationed in Reykjavik. They eventually married and after WWII, she came to the United States, where she and her husband made their home in Illinois. Over the years, they became parents of three boys and seven girls that Íeda enjoyed entertaining with many folk-tales of her mysterious homeland. The children were especially intrigued with stories of the '*Hidden People'* who were known to be helpful folks, but did not take kindly to naughty children climbing on top of lava rocks that were known to be the *Hidden's* castles!

Íeda's love and creativity in decorating her home on a small budget inspired her to enroll at Chicago School of Interior Design. After graduating, she owned and operated her own design shop. Ms. Herman wrote numerous decorating articles for local newspapers and magazines.

After retiring in 2009, and her family grown, Íeda turned her writing to her beloved Iceland, penning a memoir for her family;

originally titled *Trölls-Monster Worm-Hidden People: Fond Memories of Iceland*. Not one to stop there, Íeda enrolled, and graduated from the Institute of Children's Literature in West Redding, Connecticut and continued writing.

Other Books by Ieda Jónasdóttir Herman:

The Silver Arrow Illustrated

Inner Space Aliens (2017)

Growing Up Viking: Fond Memories of Iceland (2017) [Previously published under the title *Trolls-Monster Worm-Hidden People: Fond Memories of Iceland*]

Co-Authored with Heidi Herman
Homestyle Icelandic Cooking for American Kitchens

www.ingramcontent.com/pod-product-compliance
Lightning Source LLC
Chambersburg PA
CBHW070959120726
47910CB00004B/1299